THE PISTOLEROS

Center Point
Large Print

Also by E. E. Halleran and available from Center Point Large Print:

Straw Boss
Shadow of the Big Horn
Cimarron Thunder
The Hostile Hills
Crimson Desert
High Prairie
Warbonnet Creek
No Range Is Free

THE PISTOLEROS

E. E. HALLERAN

Center Point Large Print
Thorndike, Maine

This Center Point Large Print edition
is published in the year 2025 by arrangement with
Golden West Inc.

The text of this Large Print edition is unabridged.
In other aspects, this book may vary
from the original edition.
Printed in the United States of America
on permanent paper sourced using
environmentally responsible foresting methods.
Set in 16-point Times New Roman type.

ISBN: 979-8-89164-428-1

The Library of Congress has cataloged this record
under Library of Congress Control Number: 2024947015

CHAPTER 1:

The pack train had just moved into the worst of the downgrade when Kimbrell spotted fresh sign. He swung stiff-legged to the rocks, motioning for the men behind him to halt the mules. In the Sangre de Cristos pass caution had to be practically a matter of instinct. Kimbrell had learned the lesson on his first trips between Bent's Fort and old Fort Massachusetts. In the old days the Sangre de Christos had been dangerous because this was the border ground for Utes, Apaches, Comanches—sometimes even Lipans and Kiowas. A trade outfit could get mixed up in all kinds of troubles. Now, in the autumn of sixty-one there was a new danger. The big war in the East was making a difference. A man had to be ready for almost anything.

The tall man tied his rangy mule to a clump of junipers where the narrow trail widened a little on a ledge. Then he hunkered down for a quick study of the faint marks which had caught his attention. At least two different horses had left tracks here, both of them larger than the animal whose sign they had been seeing all the way from Fort Garland.

After a careful look he stood up again, easing some of the kinks out of long legs and glancing back along the line of mules to where a stocky little man in a pointed straw hat and a faded red serape was riding forward. Passing a mule train on that narrow shelf was a tricky business so Kimbrell made no effort to get the smaller man's attention. Esteban knew that he was wanted up ahead. That was why he was coming.

"Take a peek," Kimbrell said in English as the squatty little man slid from his dun-colored mule. "Two riders anyhow. Maybe more. Fresh sign." He had straightened to his full six feet by that time, looking even taller beside the dumpy New Mexican.

Esteban nodded and bent over to study the marks Kimbrell had indicated. "Fresh," he agreed in a hoarse growl. Then he shuffled on bowed legs toward the narrower passage ahead. Kimbrell followed at a discreet distance, making sure that he didn't interfere. He was himself a pretty shrewd tracker but in this business even Indians could not match Esteban. All the squatty man needed was room and a little time. Kimbrell would give him both.

The New Mexican practically crawled across the stretch of wider trail, studying every patch of loose gravel. He turned back when he reached the spot where the trail led among the crags. Bare rock in that stretch would tell him nothing.

"Six, I think," he reported in hoarse Spanish. "They ride to this place but turn back toward the

Huerfano. I do not know why. Maybe it is only because there is no other place so convenient for turning around."

Kimbrell nodded his agreement. "Shod ponies," he said quietly, his eyes wide open as though his thoughts were far away. The mannerism was one which often fooled people. Those pale blue eyes always seemed so innocent against the background of tanned skin and black whiskers. People simply couldn't believe that Sam Kimbrell was thinking hardest when he looked so absent-minded. With Kimbrell the wide-eyed stare was what the furrowed brow was to most men.

Esteban was one of those who understood. He grinned briefly, showing an assortment of broken and crooked teeth. "Shod ponies," he agreed, switching to English with no more accent than Kimbrell's brand. "Soldiers, I think."

The blue eyes went a little wider. "Likely some of the ones we're looking for." He didn't need to explain further. Both men knew that regular troops would not be in the region. Federal garrisons had been weakened by desertions and the resignations of Southern officers. Post commanders did not have men enough for their regular patrols, even when they put militia into service. Actually, the use of militia along the Santa Fe trail had become an added problem, some of the units deserting wholesale to become outlaw bands armed with government weapons.

For Kimbrell the thought of soldiers had to be an ominous one. The men who had left these tracks might be outlaw deserters or they might be Confederate guerrillas. In either case the prospects were not good.

Kimbrell changed to Spanish as he asked, "Any chance that these men came up here to meet the man we've been following?"

Esteban shook his head. "The other man came much earlier. The new tracks were made today, perhaps only minutes ago."

"Captain Madison's men, perhaps?"

The New Mexican grinned again. "You believe that Captain Madison is real, señor? You do not think Colonel St. Vrain is having bad dreams?"

Kimbrell shook his head. "Bad dreams, maybe yes. But dreams based on something. Colonel St. Vrain is a smart man. He learns things which the army knows nothing about—or won't believe. Anyhow, it's up to us to find out. Bring the train on slowly. I'll push on to the point where it's possible to look down into the valley. Bring my mule; I'll walk."

He didn't need to explain his purpose. Esteban would know exactly what he had in mind. It was a curious thing that two men who could converse well in two languages often needed to use neither. They simply understood each other.

Kimbrell pulled Colt's dragoon revolver from his belt as he went down the trail afoot, checking its percussion caps and loads as he took the first long strides. The weapon had not been used in months but it had been kept ready at all times. Checking it now was just one of the extra precautions which the situation seemed to demand.

The trail—such as it was—pitched sharply downward between boulders for some two hundred yards but then it emerged on an expanse of bare mountainside where it was simply a precarious shelf across a yellow gravel slope. The inevitable junipers seemed to button the gravel to the mountain but Kimbrell had no eye for such fancies today. He was studying the sign which showed plainly enough now. Six riders had come up out of the Huerfano Valley and had gone right back down again. The older tracks of the rider who had come across from the San Luis Valley were pretty well blotted out by the new marks.

He considered the possibilities, feeling sure that these men were a patrol of some sort. Not from Fort Garland, of course. The garrison there couldn't even manage to cover its own territory. Fort Union was reputed to be in even weaker condition, frantically trying to recruit militia against the Confederate threats on the Pecos and the Rio Grande. Fort Wise wouldn't risk men as far west as the Sangre de Cristos when they couldn't even put proper patrols on the Santa Fe Trail. Probably St. Vrain had been right in his worries; the Confederate sympathizers along the Arkansas had mobilized some militia units of their own. Kimbrell's job was to find out what he could about the numbers and strength of such groups.

With the hot October sun beating against his shoulders it was difficult to remember that he had a personal stake in all this, a personal stake where time was a big factor. He had to get through before the weather could change—but one way or another he had to get through.

He grimaced a little as the thought went through his mind. This was worse than in the old days of getting mixed up between warring Indian tribes. The big war had come West but nobody seemed to know just what it was going to mean to the frontier. For Kimbrell the uncertainty carried an extra bitterness because he had felt all along that none of it was of concern to him. If those idiots back East wanted to fight a war why couldn't they fight it among themselves and let other folks alone?

He crossed the open stretch to where the trail wound a serpentine course among crags. Just ahead of him was the sharp angle which marked the start of the last long pitch down to the banks of the Huerfano. From that point he would be able to see the narrow valley which marked the end of the pass. Perhaps he might even get a glimpse of those strangers who had climbed the mountain only to turn and ride back down again.

Moments later he was staring down at the little thread of river. It was not much of a river at any season but now it seemed to carry almost no water. Still it marked the bottom of the gulch and he could make out the trail beside it. He was seeing it from a distance of some four hundred yards but the direction was straight down. As he stared into the gorge he was aware of the dark clouds which were banking up in the south. From this spot he should have been able to get a glimpse of the nearer Spanish Peaks but now there was nothing in that direction but those angry black thunderheads. It was a warning that had to be heeded. The season for violent summer storms was not past and he didn't want to have the mules caught on the mountain in one of those gulley-washers which had given the Sangre de Cristos such a fearsome reputation.

Then he saw the moving figures below him. Eight dark forms crawled along beside the winding thread of the Huerfano; they were men in some kind of uniform. At the distance he could not be sure but he guessed that they were wearing government blue. While he was trying to make up his mind about it he caught a glimpse of movement farther downstream. At least three other riders were showing there, perhaps a quarter of a mile ahead of the men he had seen first. It seemed to Kimbrell that they were separating to take positions along the little river.

He hunched forward with keen interest, the pale blue eyes wide again as he tried to make out details. He didn't think that the distant trio were Indians but they did not appear to wear any kind of uniform. What really caught his attention, however, was their definite furtiveness. It seemed like a sure bet that they were preparing some sort of ambush for the eight men directly below.

He moved to a new position, trying to get a better look at the gorge downstream. It seemed to him that there had to be more of the ambushers. Even with the advantage of surprise and position it didn't make sense for three men to attack eight.

For a moment he considered trying to get some kind of warning to the nearer group but then he thought better of it. Those blue uniforms didn't mean a thing and any demonstration on his part might be misunderstood. He didn't want to attract any attention to himself and his outfit until he knew a lot more about the situation.

While he was still trying to puzzle it out, the action started. The uniformed men had moved on down the gulch until they were what Kimbrell guessed was a long rifle shot from where the other three had taken cover. Then three puffs of smoke blossomed from behind the rocks and the bushwhackers went into headlong retreat down the river. Clearly they hadn't tried to do any real damage, simply firing and retreating in a sort of crazy gesture.

Instantly the eight soldiers broke formation, spreading out to take cover but still pushing forward in a skirmish line. Obviously they had not seen the retreat of the enemy but were simply moving ahead, expecting a real attack and getting ready for it. Disciplined troops, Kimbrell decided. There was no sign of panic. Somebody had given the right orders and the men were obeying without hesitation.

Kimbrell waited until he was sure that they were not being drawn into a trap and then he turned back to meet the mule train. What he had seen didn't make much sense—and he had to wonder about the identity of the men in blue—but for the moment he had to concern himself with something more personal. Thunder clouds over the Sangre de Cristos were his immediate concern.

"Bring 'em down as fast as you dare," he told Esteban when he swung into the saddle of his riding mule. "There's a bad blow making up toward the Spanish Peaks. Seems to be heading this way. Try to reach the valley before it hits. Check all the tarps as you herd 'em along. I'm going to have a look down below. Some shootin' down there."

"Soldiers?" Esteban asked quickly.

"Who knows? In this damned mess nobody's sure who's a soldier or what side he's on. All I know is that some hombres not in uniform took some fool potshots at some who are." He was pulling away as he spoke. There wasn't any point in distracting Esteban with specific puzzles. The squatty man would need to keep his thoughts completely on mules for the next half hour or so.

Kimbrell took a longer look at the storm clouds as he rode out across the open area once more. It was useless to try guessing speed or direction. Storms in the Sangre de Cristos had a knack of being as erratic as they were violent. The elements took strange courses, sometimes seeming to lash themselves into a fury of frustration as they bounced from peak to peak. It was quite common for one small area to be battered repeatedly by the same storm while nearby areas were untouched. Kimbrell recalled the story of how one of William Bent's wagon trains had been held up for days on the edge of these same mountains because a full third of the oxen had been killed by lightning—in a storm which affected an area no wider than the tiny Huerfano valley. A man couldn't make any plans to avoid lightning but he could try to get his property into position where a stampede might be avoided.

Kimbrell tried to ignore such thoughts—and the threatening clouds—as he pushed on ahead. That job was Esteban's. His own chore was to see that the mule train didn't run into bigger trouble than the storm. He had to find out what the shooting meant, not only for St. Vrain but because it was now a very personal matter affecting his property interests.

The big mule made good time down into the gorge, Kimbrell reading sign as he rode. He found the spot where two riders had waited by the little river, evidently on guard there while the other six made their brief excursion into the higher country. That accounted for the difference in numbers which had bothered him.

Then he reached the spot where the soldiers had spread out at the first sound of firing. Now he was not so sure about the smartness of their move. The show of discipline which he had witnessed still puzzled him. Maybe the order which these men had received had been a bit rash but they had obeyed like Regulars. The reports which had come south to St. Vrain's ears had simply said that Confederate recruiters were getting active along the upper Arkansas. Kimbrell could not believe that any disciplined force could have been put together this quickly from the collection of miners and ranchers who would have been the recruits.

It occurred to him that there were a lot of things he didn't understand about this damned war. He couldn't even understand why it was being fought. Both parties did a lot of ranting about loyalty—either to the Union or to some native state—but it seemed to Sam Kimbrell that most of the gaudy phrases were intended to cover nothing but prejudices. Never having lived in a state—and with the word Union carrying only a vague meaning for him—he couldn't sympathize with the prejudices of either side. It just happened that he was a little more impatient with the South than with the North.

His New Mexican employees seemed to have similar feelings. The war meant nothing to them. For the most part they tended to side with the Union because the hated Texans were on the other side. Many were influenced—as was Kimbrell's case—by the fact that men like Kit Carson and Ceran St. Vrain were Unionists. Talk about loyalty didn't mean much, particularly when it was generally so full of sheer nonsense.

He brushed the thought aside almost as it came to him. This was no time for him to be wondering why he had let himself become virtually a spy for the Union side. He had to keep his mind on the twin dangers which his mule train was facing. He couldn't do much about the storm, but at least he could look into this fighting in the gorge.

He reached the spot where the three ambushers and their pursuers had crossed the little river to ride northward into the rolling foothills at the mouth of the gorge. There was plenty of sign and he took pains to work it all out. He saw that the ambushers had come directly upstream some time before the patrol entered the valley from those northern foothills. Now the pursuit was backtracking the patrol's original approach. Somehow that seemed a bit suspicious. Why should the retreating bushwhackers move in that direction instead of along their own backtrail?

With his suspicions aroused he risked a few extra minutes on a brief ride down the river. Almost immediately he found what he had half anticipated. At least seven men had milled around there as though in some sort of conference. Four of them had ridden off into the southeast while the other three—the ambushers—had gone up into the canyon. Now it all seemed to add up. The ambush had been just as false as it had appeared—but not as foolish. Somebody had wanted to draw those soldiers out of the gorge before the mule train arrived.

Kimbrell didn't wait to make any more guesses. The thunderheads were getting closer, the rumble of continuous thunder echoing down the gorge. It would be time enough to make some more guesses after the mules and their loads were safely down out of the pass. Esteban would need all the help he could get if this storm came on.

Still he found himself guessing as he rode upriver again. Either the ambushers were friends who were trying to lure an enemy away from the mule train or they were enemies who planned to attack the train and didn't want any interference from the soldiers. Neither alternative sounded very cheering.

CHAPTER 2:

A blast of cold from the mountains hinted that he might have spent too much time with his scouting. He had hoped that the storm might swing off to the east as so many of them did but this one seemed intent upon aiming its full wrath at the valley of the Huerfano. The clouds had baffled around at first but now the feathery wisps of gray flared out of the blackness toward him. This was going to be a bad one, probably with plenty of lightning and perhaps some hail. Those reaching wisps of gray were the skirmishers moving out ahead of the main assault column. Once the freighter had simply to worry about Indians. Now he had to be on the alert for military units which had gone outlaw.

Lightning flared under the clouds as he moved back into the narrower passage. Thunder was deafening now, following the flashes so closely that there was almost no interval between. Kimbrell knew that he had to join Esteban and the train in a hurry.

The first violent gusts of the main storm were whipping loose gravel in his face when he saw the New Mexican and the first of the mules emerging from a patch of timber. Esteban had made his miracle in getting the animals out of the pass but the job was not yet complete. This part of the gorge was too much like a funnel for comfort. Mild squalls could become howlers between those steep cliffs. He started to yell orders at Esteban but broke off without saying even a word. Instead he moved to the rear to give some assistance to a hunchbacked man who was keeping the line closed up. Esteban knew the Sangre de Cristos better than anyone else; he would be heading for the only decent bit of shelter within reach. He wouldn't need Kimbrell to tell him about it.

Rain hit them as they swung the first animals into a rocky pocket where a few ropes could form an improvised corral. Behind them a solid wall of rain was coming but there was time to make the proper moves before it hit. Then the danger of stampede ended as even the more skittish animals seemed willing to put their heads down and wait it out.

There was a minute or two of this sodden lethargy but then hail began to mix with the rain. It wasn't easy for five men to keep forty-four mules under control when the hail was prodding them into renewed restlessness, but somehow they managed it, weathering out the new moment of danger until they could relax again in just plain rain. By that time it even felt pretty good to be wet.

Like most seasonal storms of its type this one

quickly exhausted itself in its own violence. A dozen heavy crashes of lightning seemed bent on knocking a mountain or two down into the valley. There was another brief moment when big hailstones came down. Rain threatened to flood the whole gorge. Then it was over and a tiny patch of blue appeared in the west. Rain was still falling east of the pass but the storm was moving away.

Kimbrell took a good look and snapped orders for a renewed march. The Huerfano was already running almost bank full, the tons of water which had fallen into the canyon being augmented by heavy runoff from the sloping rock walls. It would get worse as the minutes passed and Kimbrell was too smart a man to let his train get caught in a flash flood.

"Move 'em out fast," he ordered. "I want 'em clear of the narrows before the peak of the flood comes down. Tell your men to drive hard but to make sure we don't have any broken legs. The footing will be slippery." Again he spoke with the knowledge that the detailed orders weren't really needed. Esteban would know exactly what was necessary.

They moved swiftly but with flood waters beginning to swirl out across the lower flats beside the gushing river. Two dangerous stretches were crossed without casualties and then they were in the clear, able to let the animals edge toward some of the foothill country at the mouth of the pass. Already there was a new crispness in the air and Kimbrell congratulated himself that the storm had come early enough so that men and animals could get dried out before nightfall. Some of the normal chill of October would probably follow the storm.

He managed to tell Esteban about the probable enemies ahead as they eased the train through mud to safer ground. "I can only guess what it means," he confessed, "and I don't like my guess. I think a man was sent up into the San Luis valley to keep an eye on things, probably on behalf of Confederate interests. He found out that we were bringing the mules through. Maybe he even got wind of the ammunition we're hauling. Anyway, he headed back through the pass ahead of us to report. It was his track we've been seeing for the past few days. I think he rounded up some friends and got ready to ambush us but the game was busted up when that patrol happened along."

"It could be the way of it," Esteban agreed, speaking in Spanish although Kimbrell had used English. "The foolish shooting was intended to draw the soldiers away before they could know that we were coming through."

"That's my guess."

"Then the soldiers are friends?"

"I'm not so damned sure. Maybe both parties are out to get us. One lot got rid of the rival crowd to give themselves a free hand. Not that it makes much difference now. Only part of one party is on our side of the river. They're the ones we've got to look out for."

"How many?"

"Four, as far as I know. There were seven but three of them did the bushwhack job and led the patrol a chase to the north."

Esteban shook his head. "Four enemies. It is bad. They can cause us much trouble."

Kimbrell grinned. Esteban was practically bragging when he talked like that. Four men weren't going to pose much of a threat.

They were well out into more rolling country, still following the swollen river but at a safe distance, when Kimbrell rode ahead, anxious to pick up any signs of danger. There would be no tracks to tell him anything now. He had to remember that the four men he had mentioned might well be only the scouts for a larger party. It didn't make much difference whether the unknown enemies were Confederate raiders or just plain outlaws, they would be mighty interested in grabbing forty-two mules and some pretty valuable merchandise.

For a good hour he probed cautiously ahead of the mule train, never losing sight of his outfit. Then the country changed and he eased back a little so that he was only a hundred yards ahead as he led them through a shallow gulch. That was when he heard the yells behind him. One of the muleteers was shrilling, "Soldados! Soldados!" The man's tone hinted that the word was not a happy one. Most New Mexicans could think of soldiers only as a source of much trouble. Kimbrell was about ready to agree with them.

A single glance over his shoulder told him that a file of riders had come out of the hills to approach the opposite bank of the swollen river. They were wearing government blue and their general appearance and manner told him that this was the patrol he had seen in the gorge. Evidently the storm had caused them to abandon their pursuit of the bushwhackers.

Suddenly he realized that now there were ten of them. It was amazing the way this outfit seemed to grow every time it appeared in sight. Ten men and two almost unburdened pack horses now.

He started guessing again even as he waved a casual salute to the still distant troopers. It seemed just as well to let them think that he was not particularly interested in their presence. He decided that they had come to the mouth of the pass and had left two men to guard their scanty supplies and the pack horses while the remaining eight went into the river gorge. Then another pair remained along the river while six made a climb into the lower pass. That much seemed reasonably certain although he could not imagine why they had been interested in such a seemingly pointless bit of exploration. Obviously they had been in the area for some time, quite distant from their base. Exhaustion of their supplies hinted in that direction. The one thing he would have preferred to figure out was their intentions toward the mule train.

They swung in beside the brawling little river, just in the rear of the mules, maintaining a neat double file as their leader seemed to be seeking a place to cross. He wasn't going to find such a place, Kimbrell knew. The Huerfano was in full flood and the usual easy fords would be impossible of passage.

In the fading light of the afternoon it was difficult to tell much about either the men or their uniforms but then the rushing torrent dashed through a brief gulley and the two parties came closer together. The river's roar prevented any exchange of shouts, but both groups could now take stock of each other. Kimbrell could imagine what the soldiers would be thinking about the five muleskinners. Esteban looked the perfect bandit. Hunchbacked El Toro—no other name known—at the rear was a fairy-tale monster. Pablo and Pedro would have been decent looking young half-breeds if they hadn't gone to so much trouble to make themselves look as evil as Esteban.

Kimbrell knew that he looked no less piratical than his men. The sun-bleached gray shirt was the only part of his outfit which wasn't Mexican. Straw hat, black pantaloons and boots were strictly Latin. With the stubble of black whiskers which covered his square jaw, he must look the real bandit chief.

Esteban came up beside him then, waving casually to the troopers who rode directly opposite. "There is something wrong there," the little man said in Spanish, not even glancing across the river again. "These are guerrillas or the army has made dragoons out of foot soldiers. I do not like it."

Kimbrell understood. He had already been considering the fact that the soldiers beyond the Huerfano were wearing infantry uniforms without any regimental insignia. At least the jackets and breeches were uniform. Sodden felt hats and miners' boots didn't quite complete the outfits. Five of the enlisted men had dragoon pistols in their belts. All had carbines stuck into regulation saddle scabbards.

"Government outfits, mostly," Kimbrell said. "Even the carbines."

Esteban hunched his blocky shoulders under the damp serape. "Much material has been stolen lately. The horse brands I do not like. None are of the government."

Kimbrell didn't reply. He was staring ahead with that curious wide-eyed look. He had to remember that the men beyond the Huerfano were not the immediate worry. An enemy was on this side of the flooded stream.

"Altered carbines," Esteban remarked after a period of silence. "Some of the old flintlocks that were changed to percussion and stored away. I think they have been sawed off to make carbines. They could be government issue."

Kimbrell glanced across the river and nodded. "You know a lot of odd things, don't you? You're right about the alterations—but plenty of government guns are in the enemy's hands. We still can't figure much on this gang."

The two parties moved on down the swollen river, Kimbrell getting some grim amusement out of the way the Ortiz twins—Pablo and Pedro—were enjoying a little game they had contrived. They kept waving happily across the river at their opposites, smiling in most cordial fashion—and yelling obscenities which could not be heard by the victims of their wit. Insulting Gringos was a game any Mexican could enjoy and now these two young rascals had their perfect opportunity. The boys were not old enough to remember the old war so their resentment of Gringos had to be something they had learned from their elders. It occurred to Kimbrell that here was a matter which had to be kept in mind when estimating New Mexican loyalties. The New Mexicans had no reason to feel very kindly toward either side in the present war.

Again he had to push his thoughts aside, knowing that he must think about immediate dangers. Those men beyond the Huerfano might be a puzzle to him at least they were on the far side of a swollen river. Somewhere on the near side was at least part of a gang which had probably planned to attack his train.

"They'll hit us tonight," he told Esteban after another interval of grim silence. "If they were friendly and trying to keep that patrol off our backs they'd have showed themselves by this time. They're lyin' low."

"Then you think the soldiers are friends?"

"What I'm figuring is that the bunch that's on this side of the Huerfano knows that they've got to take a crack at us while the other lot is still on the other side of the flood. So they'll hit us tonight."

"No problem," Esteban said with fine scorn. "Four men!"

"Could be more. Maybe the four who rode away from the mouth of the pass were going for help."

The little man's heavy shoulders came up in the familiar shrug. "We have fought odds before. We still live."

Twice as the shadows began to lengthen Kimbrell rode out ahead to scout areas where danger might lurk. Each time he made the move he motioned across the Huerfano to let the burly patrol officer know what he had in mind. Each time the officer sent three troopers ahead to provide a sort of flanking party for Kimbrell. Or were those flankers really guards? Kimbrell wished he could guess a little more accurately at the intentions of the patrol.

No enemy appeared and no fresh sign was discovered. Finally Kimbrell called a halt for the night, selecting a spot that had neither high ground nor timber near it. Any night attack would have to come across open country.

The Huerfano was far over its banks at that point so there was another advantage. The patrol camp—which was established as soon as the mule train halted—had to be at a considerable distance back from the river. Kimbrell wanted it that way. In the event of a fight he wouldn't be getting any real help from the soldiers so he didn't want to risk any wild shooting from them. Until he knew more about them he didn't propose to take unnecessary risks involving either their intentions or their good judgment.

Across the river the patrol managed to find enough dry material for fires but Kimbrell's men didn't light any, settling down for the night on cold rations. There didn't seem to be any point in providing beacons for those unknown enemies.

"We do not have long to wait," Esteban predicted when everything was ready. "Men who know this country will know that the Huerfano will fall as swiftly as it rose. They will know that daylight will show no remaining flood. They will know that the soldiers will be able to cross at that time. So they must strike early if they are to strike."

Nobody argued. When Esteban Mendoza offered an opinion it was worth hearing. He had a knack for understanding such things.

Trouble came even sooner than they had anticipated. Kimbrell was still moving around in a final check of the packs, making sure that vulnerable merchandise had not been damaged by the rain, when one of the twins hurried in silently from his up-river post. He reported that he had heard horses coming toward camp. The animals were being led rather than ridden, he thought, so he had decided to make a quiet report instead of shouting an alarm. Meeting stealth with stealth seemed like the smart move.

"Good boy," Kimbrell told him. "Esteban, get the downriver guard in. We defend the camp only but keep an eye on the other angle. They may be aiming to hit us from both sides at the same time. I'll take care of the upstream end. Leave it to me. The rest of you stay right here—and guard those mules!"

CHAPTER 3:

The tall man swung sharply away from the river, making for even higher ground than the spot where the sentry had been posted. He didn't want to let himself be silhouetted against the swollen river with those camp fires on the opposite shore to throw the wrong kind of reflections.

He didn't have to go very far. The intruders evidently hadn't heard the sentry's departure and they were moving along with no show of alarm. Kimbrell could count four of them against the shimmer of the Huerfano's flood and he could see that each man was leading his horse. The number seemed significant although he still couldn't rule out coincidence. This was the remainder of the bushwhack party.

He watched the dark shadows carefully, trying to guess their intentions. At the same time he was keeping an ear cocked for the sounds of other movement. Because there were four men in front of him did not mean that there might not be others sneaking in from elsewhere.

He moved along with the four shadows as they neared the camp, finally accepting the guess that this was the whole attack. They were depending on surprise to offset their lack of numbers. They huddled briefly as though in quick conference, then began to mount. Evidently they were not going to depend on stealth for the final approach but would drive in at full speed. At least that was the way Kimbrell guessed.

He took one more quick look at his own rear and then shouted, "Hold it, you men! Don't make a move. Who are you and what do you want?" He raised his voice so that the roar of the flood would not cover the words. Then he took a dozen quick strides toward camp, changing position simply because it seemed like smart strategy.

He had hardly hunkered down again when he knew that the move had been no mistake. A reply came swiftly, telling him what he needed to know about the intentions of the four. A gunshot blasted at the spot where he had been standing when he challenged. Another followed on its heels and he could tell by the streaks of orange in the night that they were taking blind shots at the spot from which his voice had sounded. So he triggered carefully at the dark blur of the nearest rider and moved again, still toward camp.

This time all four of them opened fire and he could hear slugs crashing on the rocks fairly close to him. They had learned fast and were firing with the expectation that he had moved. Now he saw a heavy shadow as two of the riders came into line so he aimed a little more carefully. It was time he let them know that he meant business.

He moved again as he fired but now he could have the satisfaction of hearing a grunt of pain and a string of curses. He still didn't know who the enemy was—although the swearing had carried a ring of the deep South—but he no longer need doubt that it was indeed the enemy. The fight was on.

In spite of his anger at their interference with his affairs he did not fire again even though they now gave him a fine target as two of them closed in as though to help the wounded man. He preferred to let them make another move without the prodding of further gunfire.

They made it, surprising him a bit. They simply wheeled their horses and beat a hasty retreat upstream, even the wounded man riding hard.

He listened to the dwindling hoofbeats, holding his position until he was certain that no other enemy was moving toward him. Then he headed back to camp, trying to make up his mind about things.

"I still don't know who's who or what they're tryin'," he told Esteban angrily after relating what had happened. "One guess is that these jiggers hoped to stampede our mules. Four of them couldn't hope to do a real mule-stealing job—and if they had other plunder in mind they'd have made the attack when the mules had their packs on. The whole damned affair would look plain stupid if I didn't remember that this same crowd pulled that fake ambush yesterday. That looked stupid, too, but it had a purpose behind it. I keep thinking that maybe there was an extra purpose tonight."

Esteban gestured toward the dying fires of the patrol camp. "Where does that gang fit in?"

"That, amigo, is our biggest problem. They could be a rival gang of guerrillas out to steal our mules and supplies. If that's the case they're dangerous because they're organized—and they've been smart enough to outfit themselves in stolen Federal gear. Tomorrow morning's going to be a lot more troublesome than tonight has been."

When the first light of a chilly dawn crept across the valley, the little river had passed its flood stage and was subsiding rapidly into its normal state of autumn lethargy. The patrol could cross at any time. Probably they would wait until they could find a ford less muddy than the expanse between the camps but they still wouldn't delay very long.

"We'll assume that this patrol is loyal to the Union, one way or another," Kimbrell said. "We'll welcome them as protectors—which maybe they'll turn out to be. Anything in the packs that I don't know about? Just in case they make a search."

Esteban's crooked smile was fleeting. As usual he knew exactly what Kimbrell was thinking. "The men do no smuggling this time," he said blandly. "But we have the cartridges. How will you explain them to the officer?"

"I've got a bill of sale for 'em, damn it! What more do I need?"

The heavy shoulders came up in the same old shrug. "Anyone can write a paper. I think the patrol officer may be suspicious."

"Maybe that'll be all right. If he's suspicious enough he may decide to take us right in to Pueblo while he investigates us. That way we go under guard. Not too bad, eh?"

The New Mexican's grin widened. "I should have known. I tell the others."

"While you're at it warn the boys about their tongues. Some of those bluecoats may understand Spanish. Also have them keep in mind that we're not sure what that damned patrol is trying to do. We may find ourselves in a tight, so everybody be ready for a move. I don't know what the hell kind of move it could be, but be ready."

"They understand," Esteban said shortly.

Kimbrell turned away then, moving up the river to see if he could learn anything from the sign left by the night raiders. He saw that a big redheaded officer and a pair of troopers were making a similar move on the far side of the river. The expanse of mud between them still kept them from getting close but now the big man could make himself heard, the river no longer setting up such a racket.

Kimbrell gathered that the big man wanted to know about the shooting so he answered with gestures, not trying to match the volume of the other man's shouts. He kept it up as he began to study the sign, then he turned without another look across the river and went back to his own camp.

"I nicked one, all right," he told Esteban. "There were blood spots. I hope that discourages 'em."

By the time the patrol was forming up, ready to leave their bivouac. To Kimbrell's astonishment their leader was holding what looked like a formal inspection. They could hear some of the bawled orders but mostly it was his actions which drew their attention. There was a certain pompousness about his every move which made Kimbrell wonder about him. He had been thinking that the fellow was a pretty smart leader but now he began to have his doubts. Dress parade in the mud didn't make much sense.

"He handles ten men as though he had an army," Esteban muttered in Spanish.

The patrol moved downstream in formation then, two men leading off as an advance guard with the pack animals a few yards behind them. At first the balance of the patrol remained in a column but then flankers went out. At least the parade business wasn't keeping them from making the right moves for the business they were in.

"Let's go," Kimbrell ordered. "They'll be across at the first ford. Then we'll find out a few things."

He regained some of his respect for the officer when he watched the patrol making its crossing of the Huerfano. The redhead and another man inspected the ford carefully while the flankers swung wide into some broken hills. Then three men went across, moving out to act as flankers on the east side while the original flankers came down to serve as a rear guard. There had been no sign of an enemy in the region but the moves were the proper ones to make.

The train continued without any change of pace, the patrol maintaining its lead with no show of interest in the party behind them. It was only when both parties were in open country that Kimbrell saw the move he had been anticipating. The patrol halted, advance guard and flankers taking positions where they could keep a watch on the nearest bits of cover. Then the parade-ground operations began once more, the men going through a sort of drill at the bawled commands of the big officer. It all seemed pretty useless but the results were effective enough. In spite of all the lost motion the trail became effectively blocked.

They moved ahead until they were within easy earshot of the waiting soldiers. Kimbrell decided that the only course was to pretend that he had not seen the blockade as a hostile move. So he waved a casual hand and eased his mule out ahead so that he had a thirty-foot lead on the first pack mule. "Morning, gents," he greeted affably. "Weather's a mite cooler'n it was. Feels kinda good for a change." He aimed the words directly at the ramrod straight figure of the burly officer. The man wore the single bars of a lieutenant, Kimbrell noticed.

Hard gray eyes bored at him from behind the redhead's sandy stubble. Judging by the beards of the various men it seemed certain that the patrol had been out for something over a week. Even without the beards they would have been a hard-looking crew but Kimbrell didn't have time to think about the matter. The big man was firing a volley of questions at him.

"What's this heah pahty? Where might yo'-all be goin'? What was that shootin' last night?"

Kimbrell didn't like the sound of the broad Southern accent. Maybe he had guessed wrong about this crowd, but it was too late now to do anything except follow the plan he had set up in his mind. Mostly that involved being quite truthful so he didn't have to make any hurried changes.

"It wasn't so awful hot, the shootin', I mean," he drawled casually. "Them bastards what fired at your boys in the pass took a fling at mule-stealin', I reckon. They scared off mighty easy."

That jolted the redhead. "What do yo' know about any shootin' in the pass?" he demanded.

"I watched it—from up on the mountain. Ain't figured out yet who was mad at who. Maybe I don't even care very much. My business is to handle freight so I ain't fixin' to get mixed up in any troubles that ain't my own. Mostly my trouble is mules." He grinned a little as he added, "I'm Sam Kimbrell. I handle all kind o' freight between Santa Fe and the Arkansas country. This trip it's mules from Fort Garland for Denver by way of Pueblo."

"Just mules?" the big man snapped. "Ah'd say they was mighty well loaded."

Kimbrell winked. "That's what makes a man a profit, mister." His eyes were wide open now, their innocence matched by his flow of easy talk. While he talked he was trying to size up the men who now surrounded his mule train. "You see, I got these forty-two mules for some militia outfit that's formin' up around Denver. Some of 'em from Taos, some from Fort Garland. A man don't make no money movin' mules but he could pick up an honest dollar if the mules carried somethin'. So I lined me up a couple o' deals. They're all legal and proper, if you're havin' any doubts."

"What kind of deal?" The easy drawl was gone as the big officer snapped the question. "Yo' got any papehs to show fo' 'em?"

"Sure. Freight man always has papers. It's part of the business. We don't mind showin' 'em to them as has a right to look." He kept his tone casual and friendly but the challenge was there.

The big man's frown passed quickly. "That's fair enough," he agreed. "Ah'm Lieutenant George McCall, Fust Colorado Caval'y. Ah'm out heah to see if'n theah's any rebels stirrin' up trouble."

"I reckon you found some," Kimbrell said with a chuckle. "Whoever done that shootin' yesterday wasn't real loyal to blue suits."

"Let's see those papehs!" McCall ordered. "An' meanwhile mebbe yo' bettah tell me all about what yo' seen when them bastahds was shootin' at mah boys."

Kimbrell sketched in the canyon story while he was fishing the manifests out of a saddlebag. He included mention of the tracks he had scouted and of the night attack. At the moment he had to take McCall's word for his connection with a Union militia regiment so it seemed like a good idea to stick to the truth.

By the time he had opened the oilskin packet which contained the papers he had his story told. Then he went back to the business at hand as though not much interested in what had happened earlier. "Look 'em over," he invited as he handed the papers to the big lieutenant. "All in order. Forty-two mules for Governor Gilpin of Colorado. Likely for that regiment o' yours." It was a good guess—if McCall wasn't lying. "Don't get worried if you count forty-four mules. Two of 'em belong to me."

The big man shook his head impatiently as though not interested in details—so Kimbrell fed him some more. He wanted to give the impression that he was interested in nothing except the problems of a freight hauler caught in troubles he didn't understand. "Didn't have much choice in what I picked up for loads," he rambled on, letting the words come while he tried to form some estimate about McCall's men. They were mostly young, scrubby bearded and dirty. They might well be former miners who had enlisted in a militia regiment. But that meant nothing. The Pike's Peak diggings had drawn men from both North and South. Enlistments around Denver would have attracted the Northern contingent but there would have been plenty of Southerners to have formed similar detachments in the Pueblo area.

"Forty bales of hickory shirts from California," he went on. "A few sacks of Taos flour, mostly because some of the mules didn't have full loads and it ain't right to make mules think that you're showin' any partiality among 'em. Mules get ornery enough when they got no reason to be mad at you. Then there's some Sharps carbine ammunition that I bought at Fort Garland. I'm figurin' to—"

"Ammunition!" The big man evidently had been listening without seeming to do so. "Bettah tell me about that, mistah! Who gits the ammunition?"

"Third New Mexico Scouts. It goes back to 'em next trip down."

The big man didn't seem to like the answer. He ignored Kimbrell to bawl an order at his waiting troopers. "Git their guns, men! Keep 'em covehed while yo'ah doin' it. Then pull them loads apaht. Ah wanta see every damn thing they got!"

CHAPTER 4:

Kimbrell found himself staring into the yawning muzzle of an ancient but well-polished horse pistol. Out of the corner of his eye he could see that his men were similarly covered. The big red-head had issued no specific orders so it was fairly clear that this had been planned ahead of time. A lanky youth whose yellow hair peeped comically from beneath the brim of a battered slouch hat wheeled his horse expertly and snaked Kimbrell's gun from his belt. Other soldiers were being equally efficient in disarming the muleteers.

"Git 'em movin'!" McCall ordered, breaking the silence which had marked the flurry of activity. "No tellin' when they otheh bastahds'll show up."

"Better let me tell my men what you want," Kimbrell said quietly. "In Spanish. It could save trouble."

"Keep yo' trap shet. Ah ain't takin' no chances. They'll know!"

He was right. The guns and gestures of the soldiers would have let the muleskinners know exactly what was wanted even if they had not understood the shouted instructions. With practically no delay the captured weapons were dumped into a sack and sent forward to be loaded on one of the patrol's pack horses. Then the mule train moved ahead, guards relaxing and enjoying their easy triumph.

One of the men shouted a question at McCall. "Hey, Stan! Ain't we gonna take a look at this stuff they're haulin'?"

"Lateh," the big man replied. "Ain't no rush." He didn't seem to mind the undisciplined nature of the question.

Kimbrell hadn't missed the name that had been used. It was not the one the redhead had given in identifying himself. Still it didn't seem like a smart idea to mention it. The only chance now was to wait to see what would happen next. Meanwhile there was no harm in trying to stick with the casual manner.

"Quite a squadron you've got here, Lieutenant," he observed as the redhead motioned for him to ride beside him. "Discipline where you need it but no fuss and feathers."

The big man grinned. "That's jest the way Ah aim to have it. If'n yo' friend Cap'n Madison takes a fling at gittin' yo' loose yo'll see how good these boys kin be."

That caught Kimbrell by surprise. He had made up his mind that the man who called himself Lieutenant George McCall was a smart guerrilla named Stan Something-or-other who was posing as the real Colorado officer. That was the way things had added up.

"Who's Captain Madison?" he asked after a moment's pause.

The redhead laughed. "Gonna play it dumb, eh? Mebbe Ah oughta tell yo' jest how come Ah'm namin' yo' a lyin' rebel."

Kimbrell nodded without changing his expression. "Seems like that could get real interesting—if not too complimentary. I take it you don't believe the papers?"

"Ah reckon as how yo' stole 'em from the real Kimbrell—if'n theah is such a gent. Theah's somethin' rotten somewheah, that's sho'."

"Just what I was thinking. But not with my papers. What sounds a mite fishy to me is to have a Georgia Cracker pretending to be a Colorado officer."

He had hoped that the sudden counter-attack might make the other man give himself away but instead he drew a quick chuckle. "Me and mah dam' sowbelly accent!" the redhead exclaimed. "Happens Ah'm f'm Mississippi but that don't make no nevah-minds—so don't be gittin' no fool ideas. Wheah this wah is concehned Ah'm a hell of a good Yankee!"

There was a curious mixture of humor and bitterness in the words. Kimbrell had a feeling that he was hearing truth so he probed a little harder. "I wish I could believe that, my friend. Then I wouldn't care a hell of a lot whether you believed me or not." He shook his head as he added, "Somehow it don't work out too good."

Suddenly the redhead's manner altered. "Don't figgah as how no Mississippi boy's good enough to git a Yank commission, eh? Well, damn yo', take a look at this!" This small show of good humor had been replaced by some of the pompousness which had marked his review of his troopers.

Kimbrell took the envelope which was extended to him, beginning to think that he half-understood. There were three documents in the envelope, all of them looking properly impressive. One commissioned George Stanley McCall as a lieutenant of Colorado troops. It was signed by Governor Gilpin for himself and for Abraham Lincoln, President of the United States of America.

"Gettin' mighty fancy up around Denver," Kimbrell remarked, using talk to cover his quick glance at the other two papers. "Folks down New Mexico way ain't so formal. Militia commissions just kinda happen."

"Yo' don't need to fool around an' let on yo' ain't readin' them otheh papehs," McCall said gruffly. "Go ahead. Ah want yo' to know that yo' ain't gonna be foolin' me none. We know what's up."

The second paper was a written order for Lieutenant McCall to "Ride to and beyond the Arkansas River for the purpose of investigating reports of rebel activity in that area." There was specific mention of rumored Confederate recruiting and of a mysterious agent named Captain Madison whose purpose was a puzzle.

The third paper was an authorization for McCall to commandeer such supplies as might be needed by his detachment, payment to be made by him at full market value with paper redeemable at the territorial capital in Denver. Both of the latter documents were signed by a Lieutenant-Colonel J. P. Chivington. There was no mention of any mules being expected from New Mexico.

Kimbrell started to comment as he handed the packet back, but he broke off as a yell came from one of the advance guard. Riders had appeared beyond the river.

McCall took a quick look around to make sure that his men were in their assigned positions, but Kimbrell didn't wait for him to issue any fresh orders. "Don't worry about anybody on that side," he said. "That ought to be the three men who led you off on a wild goose chase. The rest of the crowd's over here. Only four of them, as far as I know, but they're the ones to look out for."

"Don't tell me mah business!" McCall growled. "Jest think up some mo' lies as good as the ones yo' been a-tellin' me." He spurred away, pausing only to shout an order at the two soldiers who now rode guard over the mule train. The order was crisp and to the point. It reminded the man that there still might be weapons hidden on some of the mules. If anybody tried to pull off any tricks the guards were to shoot first and to ask their questions later.

Kimbrell waited until the redhead was out of earshot and talking to his advance guard. Then he turned to grin amiably at the young soldier with the frowsy yellow hair. "Better let me tell my boys what's expected," he said casually. "They've got no guns and I don't want them to do anything that you fellows can misunderstand."

The youth looked undecided but then nodded agreement. "I'll be keepin' my eye on you. Don't think you'll get clear with any tricks."

"I won't be trying. Your lieutenant may be smart but he's dead wrong about us. It'll suit us fine to have you boys take us right on up to Denver. Meanwhile I'd like to make sure that our mules don't get stampeded in any kind of attack."

"Tell 'em," the soldier said shortly.

Kimbrell shouted his orders in Spanish, watching to see whether any indication of understanding came from either soldier. When both men looked blank he added, "Keep an ear out. See if these men talk like what they claim to be. We need to know."

They moved on at the same pace, McCall out with the advance while his flankers ranged wider into the nearby hills. Apparently sight of unknown riders beyond the river had made the lieutenant wary.

Ten minutes later there was a sudden rush of movement well out in advance of the train. Kimbrell knew that three men had crossed the Huerfano and were moving as though to attack the advance guard. Probably the same three who had done the ambush job in the gorge. He wondered whether their present move might not be another feint of some sort. Likely enough they had managed to communicate with their comrades by means of signals from the hills.

He said as much to the nearest soldier and was mildly pleased to see that the man was taking him seriously, turning to stare toward the rear instead of putting his full attention on the prisoners. Then it happened. A rattle of gunfire sounded from downriver and the advance guard began an orderly retreat toward their nearest support—which was the two soldiers in charge of the pack animals. At the same time the more distant flankers began to close in toward the trail. With only three men now threatening the head of the column there would be ample strength to fight them off.

The guard at the rear of the mule train shouted his warning at that moment but Kimbrell was already turning to look in that direction. The attack strategy had seemed so obvious that he had known almost without conscious thought that the real attack would come at the rear after the demonstration in front. Now he saw six nondescript riders swinging out from behind a low butte and driving straight at the lone soldier on duty at the tail of the train.

"Support him!" Kimbrell yelled at the blond boy. "Hold 'em until that damned fool lieutenant can get back here!"

The soldier fired his carbine at long range, shouting loudly at the same time. Then he began to reload as he rode toward his comrade. It left the mule train completely alone. They were unguarded and they were also undefended and helpless.

For Kimbrell there was nothing to do but to dismount and help hold the frightened animals against a possible stampede. He could see that two flankers had swung to support the rear and that McCall had also recognized the danger. Now the men with the pack horses were holding out alone against the trio who had made the original fake, the rest of the detachment rushing to join the fight at the rear of the mule party.

Six men were doing the attacking from the rear angle while at least two others were trying to harass the outside flankers. With the three men who had apparently just recrossed the Huerfano that made at least eleven in the enemy force. Somehow they had picked up reinforcement since the original attack.

For a few minutes it threatened to be a disaster. The six attackers drove relentlessly at the two bluecoats covering the rear, no shot having been fired by either side after the single one which had served as warning. Kimbrell saw that McCall and the others could not reach the spot in time to halt the attack and it didn't seem that the two soldiers could do much about it. Having to stand there with no way of defending himself was maddening and he found himself steadily cursing the redheaded man for having placed him in such a position.

Then the raiders swept closer and one of the bluecoats banged away with his carbine. It was pretty long range for the clumsy weapon but the man was either a fine shot or he was very lucky. One of the charging guerrillas slumped to one side and then fell to the ground. The other soldier fired then and the show of defense seemed to be more than the attackers could meet. Kimbrell thought he understood. They were only local boys who'd become guerrilla fighters out of sheer bravado—because others were doing it. Charging around the country and making a lot of noise was fine—but having one of their number get himself killed was something else. That hadn't entered into their calculations. They simply whirled their horses, ignoring the bellowed orders of a stocky man in a wide brimmed gray hat, and hurried for cover behind the mesa which had originally concealed their assault.

McCall and three of his men arrived in time to make the chase look real but then they were returning to where Kimbrell and one of the train guards had gone out to look at the fallen raider. McCall seemed mighty pleased with himself. "Friend o' yorn, Mistah Kimbrell?" he asked sarcastically as he peered down at the dead man. "Too bad them bastahds didn't git yo' and yoah men away. They sho' as hell tried hahd."

Kimbrell straightened up to look squarely at the big man. "Lieutenant," he said quietly, "you are a damned fool!"

McCall's angry bellow hinted that he didn't know what to say and was just roaring to hear himself. So Kimbrell lashed at him again, this time dropping the easy tone and snapping the words out like whiplashes. "Simmer down, Lieutenant, and I'll tell you a couple of things. I've seen this dead man before. He used to work for Colonel Boone, the Indian Agent. A hot secessionist who talked too much and got fired. Also I spotted a couple of horse brands on those raiders' horses. Local ranches. Southern people."

"Jest what Ah been sayin', dammit! Yo' hoped some friends would—"

"Think a little, man! I've got mules to deliver at Pueblo. Somebody is supposed to pick 'em up here and take 'em on to Denver. Somebody from your regiment, I suppose. Now I don't give a damn whether you see us through to Pueblo as prisoners or allies but get us through! That's twice you've let a quick fake pull you out of position.

If these guerrillas are smart enough to try fakes, they'll be smart enough to take advantage of you. If you won't tend to business, then give us back our guns and let us defend ourselves!"

McCall's show of dignity was almost comic. He wheeled his horse so as to turn his back on Kimbrell. Then he boomed out in his best parade-ground manner. "Back to your positions, men! Smaht now! Let's move out!"

That was the last time he was within earshot of Kimbrell all day.

Twice during the afternoon the train moved past small ranches where settlers were trying to make a living from truck patches and the running of a few cattle. The houses were close to the Huerfano so the train passed close enough to them so that Kimbrell had a chance to look at the sign. In both cases the story was fairly obvious. Quite a few riders had been in and out of the places but no men except one deaf old fellow appeared at either place. Women and children showed themselves briefly but they did not come out to visit as they usually did. Nor did McCall make any effort to ask questions. If he noticed the tracks left by the numerous riders he said nothing about it. The man might be a good officer in some respects but evidently his pride gave him a dangerous blind spot. Kimbrell could only hope that the enemy bands in the area did not have strength enough to launch a real attack.

CHAPTER 5:

McCall picked a good camp site that night and Kimbrell found no cause for complaint. At least the big militia officer was running true to form. In matters like this he was pretty good. The camp would be safe against any form of surprise attack and sentry assignments were adequate. It was only when supper was over that the big man made the move which gave Kimbrell another surprise. He sauntered over to where Kimbrell and Esteban were talking, greeting them both calmly enough and taking a seat on the ground.

"Seems like we oughta talk, Kimbrell," he announced. "Mebbe we could untangle a few messes."

Kimbrell hid his surprise. "Suits me," he said. "What did you want to talk about?"

"Quite a few things. Why yo' been lyin' to me would do fo' a stahteh."

"I didn't lie to you."

The big man wasn't letting himself get flustered this time. "Let's think about it," he suggested. "Yo' claimed theah wasn't but seven o' them outlaws. Musta been a dozen."

"Yesterday there was seven. If you paid any attention to the tracks around those ranch houses back there you'd get a hunch about where they picked up a few recruits. This country's mostly southern in its sympathies, you know."

"Ah know. That's how come Ah'm heah. Yo' seen the papehs Ah'm totin'."

"Right. By the way, I'm assuming that they're genuine—and so are you."

"Well, thank yo' kindly." He let just a trace of irony creep into the words but then went back to his calmer approach.

"One thing kinda makes me want to believe yo'," the big man said slowly. "One o' them bastahds in the attack had his ahm in a sling—with fresh blood on it. Could be yo' told the truth about last night. So Ah'll jest git them packs examined and see how Ah feel afteh that."

He was moving with the words and Kimbrell made no attempt to follow. Searching the packs had to be expected. A really smart officer would have done it sooner.

Two soldiers were detailed to the job, the Ortiz twins staying close to make sure that everything was properly secured when the chore was done. Kimbrell didn't even watch. He was trying to figure out how he could best protect his interests for the balance of the journey.

McCall gave no sign when the search was completed. He busied himself with his men, ignoring the muleskinners. Finally Kimbrell decided to take the initiative so he walked across to where the big lieutenant was spreading his blankets a little distance from his troopers.

"A word with you, Lieutenant," he said in a low voice. "I know your men didn't find anything wrong with our packs so let's get something straight between us. I meant what I said about the way you handled that attack."

"Ah ain't askin' fo' no opinion!"

"But I'm giving one! And keep your voice down. I don't give a damn how much you strut in front of your men but I don't want you getting stupid when you're the only protection I've got. There's a ford ahead of us—just as we leave the Huerfano to cut across country. I think they'll hit us there."

McCall's anger showed in his face but he merely asked, "Who hits us?"

"Your guess is as good as mine. Maybe it's part of this Captain Madison business you mentioned. Maybe it's just guerrillas taking advantage of the war to turn outlaw. A threat is a threat when a man's trying to take care of his property." He paused before adding, "Maybe it's bigger than we think. The Rebs could be building up some kind of force in this part of the territory to join Sibley. I don't—"

"Who the hell's Sibley?"

"New Confederate Commander at Fort Fillmore—if he's there now. He was on his way to take command the last I heard."

"That's the place where that damned fool Major

Lynde surrendered to a gang not half as big as his'n, ain't it?"

"That's the place. A Texas Colonel named Baylor scared hell out of Lynde and took the post. Then Baylor went back to El Paso. Now Sibley is taking command from Baylor. A few months ago he was Major Sibley and he was the Federal commander of Fort Union. Now he's a Confederate Colonel and the word is that he's aimin' to gobble up every Federal post east of the Rockies."

"Rats!" McCall scoffed. "That's a heap o' country."

"Most of it helpless," Kimbrell reminded him. He went on to tell of the rumors and speculations that had been flying around Santa Fe. Lynde's surrender of the seven hundred regulars of the Seventh Infantry to about two hundred and fifty Texas militiamen had been a jolt to everyone in the region, even though it was recognized that the so-called regulars were largely New Mexicans who had been hastily enrolled to fill the gaps left by desertion. No matter what the excuses were it was still a stark fact that rebel forces held a good third of the territory. Baylor had even issued a proclamation stating that everything south of the thirty-fourth parallel of latitude was now the Confederate Territory of Arizona. Scouts brought in reports to the effect that the Confederacy was planning a big push to extend that territory north.

By sweeping away all Union resistance from the Rio Grande to the Platte the Union would be cut off from California and its gold. Every trade route would be in Confederate hands.

"That's crazy as hell. Theah ain't enough o' the bastahds in this country to pull it off."

"Then Confederate recruiting is no problem here?"

"That's the way Ah see it. Them as signed up has mostly gone to join up with the Missouri rebs. They ain't heah no more."

"Some of them seem to be."

"Hell! Mebbe a couple o' dozen. No mo' than that."

"Anyway, that's not what I wanted to talk about. It's the couple dozen I'm worried about now. I think they'll hit us at the ford and I've got a hunch I know how they'll plan it. Twice they've seen you put your men into a quick attack. They'll expect you to do it again. If they've picked up a bit of extra strength they might figure to get in behind the attack for a try at the mules. Confederate forces can use mules just as well as our side can, you know."

"Mistah, Ah don't need yo' to tell me mah business."

"That's a matter of opinion. What I'm asking now is that you let my men have their guns before we reach the ford tomorrow. I'll go unarmed and you can figure me as a kind of hostage, if that'll make you feel any better, but give my boys a chance to beat off an attack if your men get flanked."

Again the redhead seemed to make one of those sudden shifts in mood. "Sounds reasonable. Ah'll think about it. Wanta tell me how the land lays at this crossin'?"

Kimbrell explained in some detail, throwing in a couple of details as to where enemies might conceal themselves. Then McCall cut him off.

"We'll take care o' yo', son," the big man promised pompously. "Jest don't git so fretted up with that New Mexico talk. The only Rebs in these pahts is the passel o' outlaws we been seein'. We'll clean 'em out befo' we head east."

"Who's goin' east?"

"Us. Fella name of Grant is fixin' to bust down along the Mississippi come spring. He'll need help—but don't git in no tizzy; we'll clean out these fahmeh boys fo' we leave."

Kimbrell let it go at that. McCall was boasting and when he was in that kind of mood he didn't make much sense. Or maybe the man wasn't to blame. Somebody else wasn't making much sense if they proposed to take the First Colorado out of the territory. It could be the only force in position to block the ambitious Confederate plan which St. Vrain's scouts had reported.

The two parties moved a little before dawn, McCall keeping his march assignments exactly as they had been on the previous day. No more was said about the river crossing until they could see it ahead of them.

The advance guard made the crossing without delay and swung wide to serve as guards. There was nothing in the manner of any of the troopers to indicate that they were doing anything unusual. If they had been primed by their commander they were hiding the fact well. This was just a routine crossing being handled in a routine manner.

The attack came almost exactly as Kimbrell had expected it. Four mules had crossed the shallow river and three more were in the ford itself when a pair of rough-looking horsemen came around a bend in the trail some distance beyond where the advance guard had halted. They were firing as they came into view but they were moving at something less than the speed which would have indicated an all-out assault. Kimbrell decided that they were not very good fakers. Then his attention was distracted by the sound of other shots from the rear. The pattern was shaping up.

McCall's men made a better fake of their counter-attack than the raiders had done with their bit of strategy. For a moment or two Kimbrell was afraid that his warning had gone unheeded. Even the pack horse detail got into the chase as though trying to beat the advance guard to the fight. In a matter of seconds not a bluecoat remained near the floundering mules.

Then the real attack came—and the soldiers swung to meet it. Kimbrell counted five men coming out from behind the rocks and four others dashing into view from the protection of the sandhills. They were between the soldiers and the mule train but it was quickly apparent that they didn't see any advantage in that situation. They didn't give the bluecoats a chance to get within carbine range, simply wheeling to ride hard into the hills with no semblance of discipline or organization. The fight was over before it had even begun.

McCall was strutting more than ever when he shouted unnecessary orders for completing the crossing. He didn't come near Kimbrell until the march was well away from the Huerfano and then he eased in to hand over the tall man's gun. "Ah reckon yo're all right, mister. Mebbe this'll make yo' feel a mite bettah." Then he added, "Ah reckon as how mah boys kin handle theah job real good. Bettah than most Yanks, judgin' by what's happenin' back east."

Kimbrell did not reply, simply checking his gun before restoring it to its old place. If McCall wanted to talk he would listen but he was in no particular mood to have the man boasting about this particular incident.

Oddly enough, he found himself listening with considerable interest. McCall started by explaining his own personal ideas on how troops ought to be trained—a lot of it sheer nonsense—but he used the occasion to report on a number of things Kimbrell didn't know about the big war. The Yankees hadn't turned out to be good fighters, the redhead claimed. They'd run away in the big fight at Bull Run and they'd blundered badly at Wilson's Creek. The latter fight had halted a Confederate attempt to get control of Missouri but the Yanks had blundered when they had a chance to smash the rebel army. Maybe they were doing a mite better in the western part of Virginia where they seemed to have things under control and there were reports that combined land and navy forces were in full charge of the Carolina coasts. For Kimbrell the hard part of all this to understand was the size of the forces involved. More men had been killed at Bull Run than he had ever seen at one place in his entire life.

The lecture on how armies ought to be handled came to an abrupt halt when another yell of warning came from the advance guard. More riders were in sight.

"Damn stupid guerrillas!" McCall exploded. "They ain't got sense enough to know when they're licked. Give a man a gun and he thinks he's a soldier! How many lessons have Ah got to learn 'em?" All of his self-importance was back now. It didn't take much success to make the man mighty sure of himself. He was shouting his commands as he rode forward, sending four men to the rear to guard against any flank attack.

Esteban broke a long silence by commenting, “Perhaps he fights almost as well as he talks. An idiot but not a stupid idiot.”

Kimbrell grinned. He was watching the scene ahead. Already it seemed fairly apparent that no new attack was forming. There seemed to be five men on the trail ahead and one of them was wearing blue. The advance riders of the patrol were shouting something and it was evident that they had relaxed a little. Evidently they recognized the strangers.

Minutes later Kimbrell started to take stock of the new lot where they had halted beside the trail as though waiting for the mule train to come up. Their leader wore what appeared to be the Colorado uniform, his coat bearing the twin bars of a captain but with no other insignia. Light blue infantry pants were tucked into high boots and his hat was a flat-crowned affair that had seen better days. The other four wore no uniforms at all. One old fellow with a full black beard was clearly a mountain man, his long rifle held awkwardly across the horn of his saddle. The other two were less picturesque. Except that one of them was a middle-aged negro they were just like dozens of other men who could be found around mining camps.

“Heah’s the boss mule man,” McCall

announced loudly as Kimbrell rode within earshot. "Ah reckon as how he's gonna be plumb glad to turn the crittehs oveh to yo'. Them and the damned Rebs has been a heap o' trouble."

He turned quickly to face Kimbrell, scarcely pausing for breath as he called out, "Git oveh heah and meet Cap'n Hazard, Kimbrell. He's boss o' the scout comp'ny and he's down heah lookin' fo' yo' and them jackasses. Colonel Slough's gittin' plumb anxious to git 'em."

Still without pausing he swung back to the lean-faced officer. "Lucky Ah met up with 'em, Cap'n. They was havin' a peck o' trouble but Ah brung 'em through all right. Had three breshes with the damned Reb guerillas but mah boys druv 'em off and didn't take a scratch a-doin' it."

Kimbrell didn't lose his temper at this bold attempt to claim credit for everything. All he said was, "Glad to see you, Captain."

For a moment Kimbrell wondered whether his greeting would even get a reply. Captain Hazard was staring hard at the muleskinners as though far from satisfied about something. Perhaps the man was going to prove as difficult as McCall had already been. Or maybe McCall had already told him of his doubts.

Suddenly the lean man snapped, "Where the hell are these damned New Mexico Scouts?"

It wasn't at all the question Kimbrell had been expecting but he tried to answer casually. "Only four of them with me, Captain. And don't judge by appearances. They're damned good men."

"So I hear." The hard angles of the officer's face seemed to smooth out as he smiled.

It was close to noon when McCall took his detachment ahead, leaving the mule train guarded only by Hazard and the scouts. Kimbrell knew without being told that this was a matter of common prudence. The twin settlements at the mouth of Fountain Creek had been outlaw hangouts for many years. Now that they were merged as the town of Pueblo the outlaw flavor still persisted and there was the added complication that most of the respectable citizens had come from Southern states and would have their prejudices.

"We don't expect trouble," Hazard told Kimbrell, "but we try to be ready. Just take the mules to the post that used to be Catterson's and I'll take them from you then. I've got some Mex muleskinners hired for the rest of the trip to Denver, but it'll take a little time to round 'em up. That oughta give you a chance to unload."

"Suits me fine. What can you tell me about the gent who's running Catterson's place now? Likely I'll have to make some kind of deal with him."

"Never met him but once. Kind of a sickly galoot. Got money. Used to be in some kind of iron and steel business in Pennsylvania. Came out here for his health—and it ain't helpin' much. He was kind of thick with Governor Gilpin, which is how he happened to take on this deal for Boone. Boone levied on the post, of course, when Catterson lit out."

"Union man, I take it?"

"The loudest kind. I got a feelin' that the Governor wanted him down here on that account. Things kinda need lookin' after in this part of the territory."

Kimbrell was staring straight ahead, eyes wide. "Maybe more than you think," he said glumly. "I've still got a strong hunch that the Rebs are playin' 'possum."

Hazard shook his head. "Just between the two of us I'll tell you that they sent McCall down here because they expected him to find trouble. Stan's a good fighter and a smart hand at trainin' raw recruits but he's a mouthy sonofabitch and some folks wouldn't mind seein' him get his bumps. So they sent him down here to scout, figurin' that if there was any kind of a fight possible he'd get into it. You know how it worked out."

"Maybe you'd better talk to this new man before you bank too much on what McCall didn't find. I still think the Confederates are playing a deep game."

"I'll talk to him," Hazard agreed, "but I don't think he'll know much. He's not the kind of man that Pueblo folks would spill their secrets to."

Kimbrell didn't argue further. The river was just ahead now and he had to get ready for making the crossing. The Arkansas was not much of a river at this time of year but any river crossing had to be tackled with due care. A broken-legged mule wouldn't be much good to anybody.

Still he had a chance to estimate the changes in the settlement as the last of the string came up out of the water. In the three months since he had been there few changes had taken place but he decided that most of them had been improvements. Apparently business had not yet suffered much because of war shortages.

It was only when he got a look at the big frame building on Santa Fe Avenue that he really paid strict attention. Where once a dingy sign had carried Dr. Catterson's name there was now a freshly painted bit of art work announcing that Jonathan Ogden, Esq. was prepared to do business at that location. It was an eye-catching sign but Kimbrell didn't study it with half the interest that he gave to the young woman who stood beneath it. A man didn't see many women as pretty as that one.

Kimbrell forced himself to look in a different direction. He had to keep in mind that Pueblo might be a hostile town. Trouble was more than possible. He had seen McCall take his men into one of the numerous alleys in what was probably a brisk effort to chase out any lurking enemies. It was a reminder that war had definitely become part of the pattern of life in Colorado Territory.

CHAPTER 6:

The town remained quiet. A wagon was being loaded at a feed store. Two elderly Mexicans sat with their heads together in deep conversation at the door of a dingy restaurant. A half dozen other citizens turned to watch the mule team's approach. Everything was as ordinary as it could be. All except the girl at the Ogden doorway.

There were two people just outside of the former Catterson trading post, Kimbrell realized. One was a man who sat bundled in a heavy coat where the sunshine slanted in under the wooden awning. Hazard had said that the new owner of the store was in poor health so Kimbrell assumed that this would be Jonathan Ogden. The assumption was made without conscious thought because his real attention was again on the slender figure behind the man's chair. The girl was in the shadow of the awning but Kimbrell could see that she was a very pretty brunette. She was wearing a well-tailored dark skirt and a man's white shirt—and with a grandmotherly sort of shawl over her shoulders. The strange garb only seemed to accent the lithe curves of her slender but well-rounded figure.

Kimbrell wanted to ask Hazard about her but one glance told him that a question would be useless. Hazard was staring in surprise. Clearly the girl was a stranger to him—but just as clearly he was impressed.

At that moment McCall brought his patrol back to Santa Fe Avenue. His hasty search for signs of trouble evidently hadn't turned up anything, but he still brought his men out in proper formation for quick action. He had been putting on a bit of a show but he had been doing a good job at the same time. That seemed to be his regular style.

Now the redhead swung around with some of his best showmanship, evidently to inform Captain Hazard that the patrol had everything under control. Something halted him right in the middle of the turn and Kimbrell knew what it was. McCall had seen the girl by the Ogden doorway.

There was a split second of hesitation but then the big man was in proper stride once more. He shouted crisp orders to his men, catching them by surprise and bringing about some rather comic confusion for a few moments. He yelled them into formation, however, running them through the sort of drill Kimbrell had witnessed back along the Huerfano. Finally he brought them into a company front facing the Ogden place—and just in time to let the mules pass behind their line.

"Captain Hazard, sir. I report no signs of trouble in town." His salute was only a little overdone and he waited stiffly for it to be returned. Then he swung to face his men once more. This time he shouted one order. "Dismiss!"

His smirk hinted that he was quite pleased with himself as he told Hazard a little more loudly than was necessary. "I promised my boys time to get a decent meal before we move out. They've been on short rations evah since we had to pitch in and rescue these heah mulewhackehs." Anyone who hadn't heard him before might have assumed that he was generously giving full credit to his men. His manner proclaimed that he knew quite well that the real credit belonged on his own broad shoulders.

"One hour, Lieutenant," Hazard told him, electing to ignore the formalities. "I want your men in shape for guard duty so make sure they don't get too much tequila in that decent meal you mentioned!"

It amused Kimbrell to know that both officers were talking for show, perfectly aware that the girl was watching and listening. It would have been expected of McCall but it came as a small surprise that Hazard should play the same kind of game. Then Kimbrell realized that he would have done the same sort of thing himself if he'd had a chance.

He was uneasily conscious of the dust which covered his clothing—and of the disreputable whiskers—as he swung from the mule to face the pale-faced man in the chair. It was obvious that Hazard had not understated the case when he said that Ogden was sickly. The man was dying. Kimbrell had seen a few "lungers" since word had gone east that the mountain air was a boon to tuberculosis sufferers. He couldn't remember that any of the hopeful emigrants had shown much improvement as a result of their trip—and he was sure that he had never seen one who looked as bad as Ogden did. The man was pitifully thin, the skin of his hands and face seeming almost transparent in its lifelessness. Only the flashing black eyes hinted that there was still a spark of energy there. Kimbrell had a hunch that he was looking into the eyes of a fanatic but he didn't waste time in such speculation.

"Mr. Ogden?" he greeted abruptly. "I'm Sam Kimbrell. I've got some goods consigned to Colonel Boone with Dr. Catterson named to accept them for him. I understand that there'll have to be some changes made in that."

Ogden didn't try to get up. He simply gestured with one of those lifeless hands and said, "I've heard of you, Mr. Kimbrell. Colonel Boone spoke of you and left instructions. I don't think we'll have any trouble in working things out." Then the thin voice took on a harsher tone. "The flight of that rebel thief will cause complications, of course, but we'll make proper arrangements for everything."

"Good. Let's get right down to business."

Kimbrell was feeling just a little smug that his quick move had left the two officers out of the picture. Both had dismounted but they now stood and waited, Hazard's scouts apparently having gone to join McCall's troopers.

The mule train was passing the store now and Kimbrell shouted an order to Esteban. "Take 'em right into the corral! The usual place." Then he turned to Ogden once more. "Sorry if I seem to be pushin' a mite. It happens that I've got two kinds of merchandise this trip. The mules are for delivery to Denver and they're movin' on north as soon as Captain Hazard and Lieutenant McCall can get organized. The other merchandise is mine and I've been using mule merchandise to haul it." His grin was intended to let his hearer know that he was being slightly facetious, but he had an unhappy feeling that any grin with those whiskers would be something less than attractive. "So I want to get my stuff unloaded pronto. You've got storage room, I suppose?"

"Plenty." Again the harshness was in the weak voice. "The scoundrel left us practically nothing else."

"You'd better come along with me, Mr. Kimbrell," the girl broke in. "We'll attend to the problem at once." There was a hint of amusement in her tone even though she kept her face completely serious. Only her eyes betrayed her. She apparently was quite aware that men had been bidding for her attention. Which wasn't surprising, Kimbrell thought. A girl as pretty as this one would have had such a thing happen quite often.

"My daughter Alice," Ogden said quickly, half apologizing for not having performed an introduction sooner. "Mrs. Ogden will be inside of the store somewhere. Between them they manage to do the things that I find myself incapable of doing."

"Take it easy," Kimbrell told him. "We'll manage fine." Then he was following the girl into the gloomy interior of the place, leaving Hazard and McCall to stand helplessly by the hitch rack. It was a nice feeling to know that McCall was getting paid off a bit for his bumptiousness and bragging but it was nicer still to anticipate having a good reason to be with Alice Ogden. He even liked the sound of the name.

For a moment or two, his eyes balked at the interior darkness, but then he saw that the big room was notably bare. A matronly woman with dark hair piled high on her head was seated at a big desk in one corner, but there was nothing in the store itself to hint that there would be much desk work. There was almost nothing there to sell.

"You can see that we took over a store with practically no merchandise in it," Miss Ogden said over her shoulder. "That's why we were looking forward to your arrival. Colonel Boone said that you would be our best chance for some re-stocking. Apparently he was just a little too optimistic."

"Maybe not," Kimbrell replied. "I've got twenty-five wagons coming up out of New Mexico. This mule deal was something extra."

By that time the woman at the desk had turned to look at him. Her glance was one of frank appraisal but there was nothing particularly critical in it. This was obviously Mrs. Ogden. She had the same dark eyes and tilted nose as her daughter, perhaps some of the same amusement behind her calm glance.

"So this is the freighter Colonel Boone told us about," she remarked, not waiting for any introduction. "I didn't know Indians grew such horrible crops of whiskers." Somehow the words didn't seem to be particularly uncomplimentary. She was just offering a comment.

"I'm not an Indian," Kimbrell told her, thinking that Colonel Boone must have been doing a lot of talking lately. First Captain Hazard and now the Ogdens. Not that it mattered, of course. "It just happens that I lived with some Indians until Mr. William Bent took me with him to live."

"Who gave you the name of Kimbrell?"

Alice protested in some embarrassment. "That's hardly polite, Mother. Mr. Kimbrell isn't here to—"

"Never mind," Kimbrell laughed. "I'm not easily offended—and there's nothing in the question to offend me. Kimbrell appears to be my true name. All the evidence points that way."

"I like to be frank about things," Mrs. Ogden hurried on. "We always ought to know something about the people with whom we're dealing."

Kimbrell motioned toward the front door where Jonathan Ogden's querulous voice kept repeating certain phrases like damned rebels, dirty secessionists, black-hearted traitors. "I'll match your frankness, ma'am. You're going to be dealing with Southern sympathizers if you have enough customers to stay in business. That kind of talk won't make you any profits."

Alice asked a question. "Do you recommend that we hide our loyalties in order to do business—if and when we get anything to do business with?"

"No concealment necessary or useful. I don't suppose there's a person in this part of the country who doesn't know where you stand. My guess is that most folks would like to see the war stay right where it is—back in the East. They'll try to get along with people who don't agree with them if those people will play the game the same way."

"That comes strangely from a man who has been attacked several times in the past few days!" Alice showed a little more feeling this time.

"That's different. We were attacked by men who have decided that the war should be carried on actively. I don't believe you'll find that true of people who might become customers. Anyway—"

"So let's stop arguing and get business done here before all of us get angry at each other!" Mrs. Ogden's interruption was crisp but she was smiling. "Let me show you the letters we have from Mr. Boone. Then we'll get on with whatever needs to be done."

Kimbrell explained the complicated nature of his present errand as he glanced through the papers she handed across to him. It took only a few minutes to work things out then. The Ogdens were empowered to accept shipments for Boone and Kimbrell agreed to turn over to them the merchandise he was hauling as a personal venture. They were to handle it as his agent. That was the way it had been with Catterson in the past. Now the Ogdens would simply be substituted for the dour Catterson. Which would have to be a big improvement any way you looked at it, Kimbrell thought.

"We'll put the shirts over there by the door," Mrs. Ogden decided. "I'm sick of looking at those empty shelves. The flour will have to be stacked in bags on the counter by the back door." She turned as though to get back to the desk. "I hope those wagons of yours won't be long in arriving.

It's depressing to be operating an empty store."

Kimbrell caught Alice's motion for him to follow her out to the corral but paused long enough to ask, "How much have you folks sold since you took charge, ma'am? If you don't mind my asking, that is. I just happen to remember that stock was always plentiful here." He was thinking of the days—only months ago—when the shelves had carried clothing of all sorts, tools, guns, ammunition, Spanish craft work from Mexico, harness, household goods of all sorts from the east—not to mention Indian items which always could be sold to newcomers.

"I know exactly what you mean," Mrs. Ogden said, eyeing him sharply. "We're down to a few bits of leather work, some women's clothing and a few remnants of cloth—along with some items of tinware and crockery that no one ever wanted. We have no food supplies, no firearms, no powder or ball, no tools, no male clothing or shoes. Quite significant, isn't it?"

"And it was this way when you arrived?"

"Exactly. Mr. Ogden has reported the circumstances to the Governor, of course." It struck Kimbrell as mildly odd that she should refer to her husband so formally when everything else about her was informal and to the point. He didn't waste time with the thought, however. Instead he asked, "Do you draw any real conclusions?"

It was Alice who replied to that one. "Naturally,"

she said in a tone which blended impatience and curiosity. "We feel that Doctor Catterson sold everything hurriedly before disappearing with the money—which for the most part did not belong to him. We are also convinced that the sales were made to someone interested in getting supplies for a military organization, probably guerillas or rebels of some sort. And that is what my father reported to the Governor."

Kimbrell realized that both women were studying him closely. He had asked his questions in a manner which had stirred their curiosity. Under the circumstances that was bad. It didn't make any difference that their loyalty was probably beyond question; he simply couldn't afford to have anybody getting too curious about his interests.

"Sounds like a mighty interestin' sort of deal," he said casually. "Ever since I came out of the Sangre de Cristos and met that McCall jasper I've been hearing talk about rebels organizing in this part of the country. Seems to me that anybody who's interested in finding those rebels ought to dig back and find out who bought the stuff from Catterson. Where did it go? Who put up the money?"

"Would you be planning to ask those questions?" Alice asked, the strange note still in her voice.

"Me, ma'am? I'm just a freighter who got

himself caught in the middle of this mess. Maybe I'm a mite too nosey or I wouldn't even be thinking about it. Why don't you prod those two militia officers out there? That's their line of business, not mine."

He motioned toward the back door. "I've got to get busy unloading, ladies. Those borrowed mules have served their terms."

Miss Ogden gave him a steady glance from beneath neatly arched brows and he felt sure that there was a trace of disappointment in the dark eyes. She didn't say anything, however, simply leading the way out into the cool afternoon sunshine where Kimbrell's men were already unloading the first of the mules.

The corral was really a courtyard behind the store, adobe walls flanking it on the side toward the street and a series of sheds and small warehouses completing the enclosure on the other angles. Kimbrell's first glance told him that the whole pace was as empty as the store. He guessed that the stables beyond the wall would be in the same circumstance.

"I'm afraid I'll have to ask you to have your men handle everything," the girl said quietly as they moved into the open. "We have not hired any help. Until now we didn't need any."

"No problem," Kimbrell told her. "There's not enough stuff here to strain anybody. And maybe I can persuade some of those loafers to lend my boys a hand. They'll generally exert themselves in a mild fashion if they can see drink money ahead." He pointed to the half dozen loungers who had come to the corral gate to stare.

"Very well. We'll arrange terms later. Please have them bring all bales of clothing and bags of flour into the store. The two cases of ammunition which you mentioned will have to be your personal responsibility. I don't believe we should take them into the store."

"Suits me. Is the third adobe over there still sound overhead? We generally unloaded stuff like ammunition in there for Catterson. I see the padlock's still on the door."

This time she smiled. "On this one I anticipated you," she said in mild triumph. "Here is the key to the padlock."

Kimbrell grinned. "I'm beginning to think that the Ogden ladies are a pretty smart pair. Now start tallying and I'll try to round up a bit of extra help. At least two of those loafers look able to work."

What he was actually thinking was that two of the loafers looked as though they had been on the trail for some time. Possibly they had been down along the Huerfano for the past few days. Possibly they were now trying to find out a few things about the freight outfit they had tried to capture. It wasn't an idea which Kimbrell wanted to share with Alice Ogden.

CHAPTER 7:

He put on his best air of carelessness as he walked across toward the gap in the adobe wall. The two elderly New Mexicans he vaguely remembered from other trips to Pueblo. They were the regular loafers, oldsters who seemed to feel that nothing could get accomplished in the settlement unless they were on hand to watch. Kimbrell merely nodded to them, putting his attention on the other four. A lean, lantern-jawed man with a fresh crop of grizzled whiskers and a slightly heavier fellow in denim pants and a stained buckskin shirt were the two he had noticed first. So he pretended to be addressing two New Mexican youths who stood back a little behind the others. "I'm offering half a dollar for maybe twenty minutes work. Two men. Any takers?"

"Unloadin'?" the lantern-jawed man asked.

"And carrying the stuff inside."

"I'm yer man."

"Good. The hunchback will tell you what to do." He didn't even take a second look at the man he had hired, turning to glance at the pair of youngsters. It was clear that the man in buckskins didn't want to hire out so Kimbrell beckoned to one of the New Mexican youths, guessing that neither of them would push forward while the Anglo stood in front. A lot of the New Mexicans were that way. "You, Chico? Want the job?"

The boy grinned and came toward him, a little too obvious in the way he avoided getting close to the silent American. Kimbrell reminded himself that "Buckskin shirt" was a fellow who should be investigated a little. For some reason he seemed to be inspiring a certain amount of fear or dread.

Kimbrell went back to stand at the doorway with Alice Ogden as she kept a tally of the goods being brought to the store. "One thing we didn't discuss," he commented. "The pack saddles and other gear are mine. I'll need to store them until the wagons arrive. Same place as the ammunition?"

"Help yourself. As you've noticed, we have plenty of room."

"Another thing. I used to have an arrangement with Catterson to use a room at the stable when I had to stay in Pueblo overnight. Is it—?"

"Same answer. The place is empty. Probably dirty. Certainly not a very fine lodging. You could—"

"Right now all I need is a place to get a bath and a shave. If the sleeping accommodations are no worse than they used to be I'll do all right."

She was smiling faintly as she reached into a jacket pocket and brought out another key. "Padlocked," she said tersely. "I thought perhaps you might have plans like that. Will your men be there also?"

"El Toro, perhaps. That's the hombre with the crooked back. The others undoubtedly have cousins in the settlement. New Mexicans always have cousins everywhere they go. Generally female."

Hazard and McCall came out of the trading post then to break up a conversation which was just getting on a reasonably friendly footing. McCall started to put on his pompous act but scarcely uttered a word when Hazard cut him off. "I've been talking to Mrs. Ogden, Kimbrell," he said. "I gather that you see some significance in the amount of merchandise our friend Catterson sold before he lit out. You know the place. What can you tell me about quantity? How much stock did he carry?"

"Generally the place was pretty full."

"Don't duck the point! Was there enough stuff on hand to outfit any sizeable force? I'm talking about supplies that the Rebels might use."

"Clothing and shoes for fifty to a hundred men—if they happened to need the sizes on hand. Maybe forty or fifty guns of one kind or another. Not many cartridges but quite a bit of powder and lead. He dealt with trappers and Indians, you know."

Hazard nodded. "But nothing to mean much to this imaginary regiment you seem to think is holed up around here somewhere."

Kimbrell shrugged. "Not enough for a

regiment," he agreed. "Not even enough for a full company. And maybe that's one reason why the Rebels are lying low."

"Still believe they're around, eh?"

"I sure do."

McCall managed to get in a word finally. "Mistah Kimbrell ain't got much of a haid fo' figgahs," he announced with a smirk. "Can't count moah'n seven, Ah reckon. Cap'n, it's mah guess that we jest been fightin' with all the Rebs that's in this paht o' the country."

Kimbrell didn't argue. "Take a look at the man in the buckskin shirt at the corral gate," he suggested. "One of the men who made the feint at the crossing was wearing a shirt like that. You were a lot closer to him than I was. Maybe you'll recognize him."

He didn't look toward the gate as he spoke so it took McCall's scornful laugh to tell him that something was wrong. There was no longer any man in buckskin at the gate.

"Kimbrell," McCall said with cheerful sarcasm. "Yo' keep imaginin' things. Mebbe this gent is like them Rebs. Yo' dreamed him up."

Miss Ogden was smiling now and that was enough for Kimbrell. He wasn't going to get in any foolish argument, even though he had a feeling that the girl would have noticed the man and would back him up in his statement that such a person existed. Abruptly he turned to where the Ortiz twins had just sent the last sack of flour into the store.

"Get the boxes," he ordered in Spanish. "Bring 'em over to the room that's got the padlock on it. After that we'll put the rest of our gear in the same place."

He went across to remove the padlock and to peer briefly into the darkened room. He knew that both officers were watching him now. The lantern-jawed man wasn't missing anything either, even though he was still pretending to be busy collecting pack saddles, ropes, etc. Now was the time to put on his act.

"Put the boxes near the door and we'll shove the other stuff behind them," he told the boys. "I'll want to take a look into both cases. Could be we've got a bit of water in there from that storm." He spoke in English this time, loudly enough so that the others could hear him. Then he went back to where Alice Ogden was laughing at something McCall had said, repeating the bit about possible water damage as explanation for his request to borrow a hatchet.

By that time several men, obviously New Mexicans, had appeared at the gate and Hazard was going toward them, evidently organizing his crew for the march north. Kimbrell looked to see whether the man in buckskins had turned up again but then he went on with his business, carrying the hatchet which Miss Ogden had secured from a box beside the door of the building.

This time his orders were given in a low tone as the Ortiz boys brought the boxes to the storeroom. After that Pablo followed him into the place while Pedro stood guard at the door. It was obvious that everyone was interested in the move but that was the way Kimbrell wanted it.

He opened both cases, knowing before he did so that the boxes were virtually waterproof and that no rain would have even penetrated the tarpaulins which had covered them. Then he put the lids back on again, making sure that the nails didn't enter the wooden sides. Now the boys wouldn't have to risk making any noise by pulling nails in the dark.

"Transfer the cartridges into sacks that you can carry on your saddles," he told Pablo. "Bring some rocks and old rags to fill the boxes. Then ease the nails back into the proper holes before you leave. I think maybe we'll get some action out of this. Did you get the rest of your orders from Esteban?"

The boy grinned in the gloom. "We know what to do," he assured Kimbrell.

"Good. I'm depending on you. Make your move a little before midnight. Not too soon because somebody may be watching. And not too late. I want you well on the trail south by daybreak."

The boy nodded his understanding and followed Kimbrell out into the open. For the next few minutes everybody seemed to be busy. Kimbrell's crew, including the extra hands, set at the business of getting gear stowed away in the storeroom while Hazard was shouting irritably as he tried to organize his new crew of muleskinners. Apparently he had not located as many men as he wanted and he was arguing with McCall about having some of the troopers handle mules. Finally it ended with the older man shouting a direct order. "Go get 'em, dammit! Give that gang of cut-throats another half hour and they'll all be so damned drunk that the mules will have to ride herd on them! Hustle it up, we're leaving in twenty minutes!"

Kimbrell waited for a lull in the frantic milling and then made a show of snapping the padlock back into its hasp and pocketing the key. It seemed like a good idea to let everyone know that he was taking plenty of care with those wooden boxes. Their contents would certainly be no secret by this time.

Then he waved his helpers around him, paying off the two volunteers without seeming to give either of them a second glance. After that he joked with his regular crew as he handed out cash, warning them that they would have to be ready to ride in two or three days. The move let him accomplish two things. He slipped the padlock key to Pedro and he let the impression get around that his party would not be leaving town for a few days. That would afford some degree of safety for the men who would ride out tonight and might make his own next move a little easier. He had to assume that an enemy which had known about the arrival of the mule train would also have information about the wagons. For that reason he had not bothered to deny that the wagon train was on its way north. Denial would only have aroused suspicion and it seemed better to make it appear that he was not much concerned. What he needed was enough delay so that he could meet Vasquez and the others before any attack could be made on the train. By that time he hoped to know more about the strength of the enemy.

He went back into the store as soon as his men left the corral. Alice Ogden had already entered and was working with her mother in making the various bookkeeping entries which the deals required. It was the older woman who looked up pleasantly to state, "We'll have everything ready in just a moment. Meanwhile—and before I forget my manners any further—we'd like to have you stay to supper with us. Alice and I still manage to do decent cooking even though we try to act like business women."

"Thank you," Kimbrell replied. "I appreciate the offer but I'm afraid I'll have to turn it down. I've got another visit I must make without delay.

A rather disreputable customer over in Fountain City, I'm afraid—but a customer. For goods in the wagons, incidentally."

"You needn't make excuses," the woman told him, still smiling. "I suppose you have ample reason to suspect our kitchen skills."

"Believe me, it's not that. I'd like nothing better than to visit with you—with or without a meal—but time is important to me right now. Incidentally, I'd like to have receipts for the goods I brought on Colonel Boone's account. If you'll just hold those receipts for me I'd appreciate it. My personal merchandise can just go on your books to my credit."

Alice looked up then. "You seem to put a great deal of trust in us, Mr. Kimbrell."

"Not much risk, I reckon. It's a better bet than carrying valuable papers with me where I'll be going tonight. Which maybe doesn't sound very complimentary to you folks but that's the way it works out."

"You will be in danger?"

He liked the frank concern in her glance but decided that this was no time to make anything of it. "Everybody's in danger nowadays. And that includes you folks. Better keep it in mind. Now where's the key to that stable room? It's time I got some of the dirt and whiskers off."

"The place is not locked," Mrs. Ogden informed him. "We haven't had a chance to do anything about it and we haven't used it. I'm afraid you'll have company you won't like. I'm sure there must be rats."

"I'll try not to scare 'em," he said solemnly. Then he headed for the back door. It would have been pleasant to stay around a little while but he had to count his hours. He had to count them even though he didn't yet know how many of them he might have.

At the back door he almost collided with Jonathan Ogden. The man was using a cane but evidently had been able to walk around from the front to watch the departure of the mule train. His frown suggested that he did not like what he was seeing and Kimbrell could sympathize. McCall's men had done a most efficient job of getting drunk in the short time that had been afforded them. Two of them were barely able to stick in their saddles and the others were scarcely better. Only one of Hazard's detachment had even appeared, giving McCall an excuse to retort when Hazard accused him of being a lax commander. Between insults both of them were bellowing orders which brought no results worthy of mention.

Kimbrell saw that the hired muleskinners were solemnly enjoying the farce. A New Mexican enjoyed nothing more than seeing Gringos make fools of themselves, so the muleteers compounded the confusion by becoming very stupid, failing to understand even the simplest of Hazard's commands. This was the game Kimbrell had seen played many times. When a New Mexican seemed most stupid was when he was gloating at his own superiority over the blatant Americano he was annoying.

"Disgraceful!" Ogden exclaimed. "Those men are not fit to wear the army's blue! I'll write Governor Gilpin and—"

"Don't bother," Kimbrell broke in quietly. "These are the pick of the regiment, I imagine. At least they're better trained than most militiamen. And they fight real good when they're sober."

Ogden sputtered angrily at the defense as well as at the scene in front of him so Kimbrell simply raised his voice, shouting orders in Spanish to two of the New Mexicans he knew by name. "Alvorado! Miguel! Please to take the mules away from here, amigos. It would be well to herd the drunken soldiers along with the other mules. Earn your money, *companeros*!"

The gibe at the soldiers was good for a sudden laugh and then the swarthy rascal Kimbrell knew only as Miguel took charge. He yelled at his countrymen and quickly some semblance of order began to develop. The mules became untangled and started filing out through the corral gate. Hazard was quick to take advantage, practically driving McCall and his men ahead of him just behind the mules. The final bit of comedy was provided by the delighted Miguel who had gone back to playing the stupid role again. He managed to get tangled up so that everyone else was out of the corral before he was ready to move. Then he put on his show. He was indicating to Kimbrell that he—Miguel—was herding men and officers as well as mules. Kimbrell waved him a salute of acknowledgment. That little joke ought to keep the muleteers behaving themselves all the way to Denver.

Ogden seemed to sense a part of the comedy but he clearly didn't like what he suspected. "What did all that mean?" he snapped. "And how did you do it? What did you tell that peon?"

Kimbrell started toward the inner passage that would lead him to the stable area. "I understand Mexicans," he said over his shoulder. "At least enough to know that I'd never get much out of a man like Miguel by calling him a peon." Then he moved on across the corral without giving Ogden a chance to ask more questions. He didn't think that the newcomer to Pueblo would appreciate the humor of the Spanish dialogue and he didn't feel like starting any fuss with the sick man. Ogden and his trading post might turn out to be important in the months to come; there was not much sense in starting a quarrel with him.

CHAPTER 8:

The stable was just what could have been expected of a place that had been unused for some months. The only animals in it were the two mules which El Toro had brought around as soon as the unloading started. The dust was a little thicker than usual but otherwise the place looked normal. Catterson hadn't even removed the ragged blankets which Kimbrell had never cared to use. And there was a small supply of gnarled firewood behind the tiny sheet-iron stove.

He built a fire and brought in water to heat in a bucket before getting his saddlebags from the outer room where El Toro had placed them. A clean shirt and underwear would make him feel a little better although he had a hunch that it was a waste of time to get cleaned up before the night's action. Probably he would be the cleanest man in Fountain City this evening.

He was stripped and scrubbing when Esteban sidled in, a frown on his dark features.

"Troubles?" Kimbrell inquired briefly without pausing in his efforts.

The blocky shoulders came up in a regular Mendoza shrug. "Troubles. Puzzles. I do not know which. Perhaps both. Our people tell me that as many as five hundred men have disappeared from the mines and the farms—not counting those who have joined at Denver with the Governor's troops. What has happened to these men is the puzzle."

"Then they may still be in these parts or they may have gone south? Is that it?"

"That is it. No one knows."

"Your people make some mighty shrewd guesses. What do they guess?"

"To me that is the big puzzle. They cannot even guess." He dropped into a wooden chair which had been made of packing boxes. "So what do we tell our man to report when he sees Colonel St. Vrain."

"You found somebody you can trust on all counts?"

Esteban let a small grin replace his worried frown. "Paco is half Ute. He will get through without trouble. Also he once served with Colonel Carson and the Ute scouts. He will be loyal and intelligent. But we must not send a false message."

"Right. So tell him how the puzzle reads. Let him report it that way. Either McCall was right and there is no substantial Confederate force in the territory or something mighty important is afoot. Keeping this thing secret hasn't been easy. Somebody—if my guess is correct—has gone to a lot of trouble to hide this gang of recruits and to make a lot of moves to make it appear that only a few trouble-makers are riding around doing petty mischief. A plan like that could mean real trouble ahead."

Esteban got up again. "It is enough," he said shortly. "I tell him to repeat it that way. He will leave an hour after sundown. I will continue to seek information until it is time for me to join the others." Suddenly he wheeled to add, "I forget! There are men in town who have been riding south of the river. They came in an hour before we did. Also it is reported that two wounded men are now at a ranch perhaps ten miles east."

"Sounds interesting. Is one of these gents a medium stocky jasper wearing a buckskin shirt?"

"There is one such. His name is Cragg. Edward Cragg. My people tell me he is not known to them."

"Maybe he's Madison."

"It is possible. What we must heed is that our enemies still have much interest in us."

"Or in our wagons. Tonight I'll try to pick up more information but mostly I'm going to be trying for delay. You know the plans for making your move south. I've primed the Ortiz boys. Let them handle the business of getting the cartridges out of the storeroom. They're good at it. You and El Toro stay here at the stable with the horses. You did get horses, I suppose?"

"Very good horses, amigo. Hidden by my

friends when men like Zan Hicklin wished to buy and others tried to steal."

"So Zan's in on this, is he? I might have known! Funny nobody has mentioned his name."

"The Ogden people did not know?"

"Didn't know what?"

"That Zan Hicklin bought much of the stock from Doctor Catterson just before the doctor left."

Kimbrell stared. "Dammit, Esteban, how much more are you holding back? That could be important. Hicklin's neck of the woods could be just the place for a sizeable force to be hiding out. If he's supplying them he'll have left at least a bit of trace."

He was silent for a full minute as he worked vigorously at lathering his whiskers. Then he asked, "What else did you forget to tell me?"

"No more, señor."

"Then get on your way. I'll try to keep our friends interested at O'Casey's cantina this evening. It should keep them clear of you and the boys while you're making your move. Be careful."

"And you, amigo. Trust no one at the cantina. Of my own people only the worst go there. As to the others—"

"I know. I've been there before."

Dusk was settling over the sprawling settlement when Kimbrell mounted his mule and headed across toward Fountain Creek and the riff-raff hangouts beyond it. He carried only enough money for the few drinks he would be expected to consume and his revolver. When any man went to O'Casey's place he needed such precautionary aids. Now that war had complicated the already rowdy picture, the risk was greater. Still Kimbrell would have made the visit even if he had not had legitimate business to discuss with the estimable O'Casey. The cantina had long had a reputation as being headquarters for half of the villainy in the upper Arkansas Valley. Perhaps it still would be functioning.

A dozen men, most of them dirty and smelly, crowded around the plank bar when Kimbrell entered. Several of them knew the freighter by sight and promptly began to fire questions at him. He waved them off, using the confusion as an excuse. The volley of questions made it clear to him that somebody had been doing a lot of talking. The various attacks on the mule train had been pretty well reported.

That part was not what interested him most. Both of the men who had been at the corral during the afternoon were now in the cantina. Along with three or four others they were asking no questions, but it seemed to Kimbrell that they were awaiting answers just a bit more anxiously than were the actual questioners.

The arrival of Mike O'Casey from somewhere

at the rear of the bar gave Kimbrell a chance to ignore the questions a little longer. O'Casey had been running this cantina ever since the days when only a few trappers, a sprinkling of prospectors and the usual fugitives from justice were his customers. No one seemed to know what had brought the fat Irishman to the mouth of the Fountain in the first place but apparently it had suited his purposes. He catered to all kinds of thugs but somehow managed to maintain a reputation as an honest citizen. And he kept something like order in the place most of the time, his vast bulk deceptive. O'Casey was as hard as the Arapaho war club which he kept behind the bar. Legend said that he had killed at least a dozen men in his efforts to halt the periodic riots which broke out in his place—and he had lost one eye and two fingers in the same cause. To Sam Kimbrell he was a regular customer. Few wagon outfits came up out of New Mexico without hauling a few barrels of Taos Lightning for the big Irishman. Vasquez was supposed to have a dozen barrels of the stuff in his wagons this trip.

"Where the hell's my licker?" O'Casey bawled above the din. "How in hell can a man make a livin' when you damned freighters don't deliver stuff?"

Kimbrell repressed the smile which wanted to come. He knew that O'Casey was sounding belligerent by choice, deliberately giving him a chance to get his bearings before answering questions, but the man had done better than he had intended. He was giving Kimbrell the perfect opportunity to throw in some of the misinformation that might be important to him.

"Keep your shirt on!" he growled in reply. "You never change it anyway! Just put more water in the stuff you've got on hand. You always do!"

That brought a howl of approval from the customers and Kimbrell added, "Wagons ain't likely to get through for a month yet. All kinds of damned troubles on the trails."

"Like ye just had?" the fat man asked, understanding that Kimbrell was ready to talk.

"Mebbe. A man don't know what to think. Two packs of damned fools start warrin' with each other and they think they've got to get everybody else into their private feud. I've been attacked by bandits, arrested by popinjay soldiers, and skinned by a crooked trader. I'm gettin' sick of the whole rotten business!"

He noted an exchange of glances between the buckskin-shirted man and another fellow that he had not seen before. For a moment he thought that one of them might throw a question at him but for a moment or two there was only silence in the room. The men who most wanted to get information from him were content to wait for others to do the questioning. It seemed to

Kimbrell that this was part of a pattern. These fellows were being just a little too cautious for him to believe that they were not hiding something mighty important.

When the questions began to come again Kimbrell answered them, reporting exactly what had happened along the Huerfano but making sure to give the impression that he did not consider any of it to be a real part of any war pattern. To him the men who had attacked his mule train were simply thieves who wanted to steal mules. The soldiers who had captured the train and had brought it to Pueblo were fools, prancing buffoons who thought they were playing war, carried away by a sense of power, and idiotic enough to be ignorant of the fact that they were capturing their own mules. He alternated ridicule and bitterness to the point where he felt that he was being pretty convincing.

Then somebody mentioned a name. Did Kimbrell think that the men who had attacked him could be the followers of Captain George Madison. Again Kimbrell played his chosen role. He didn't know anything about any Captain Madison and he didn't want to. A bandit was a bandit and it didn't make any difference to Sam Kimbrell whether he carried a title or not.

He had two drinks as the talk went on, keeping a wary eye out to see that the liquor didn't come from one of the regular barrels. O'Casey's wink seemed to reassure him on that point. Good customers would be properly served.

After a while the general conversation eased off, Kimbrell watching with interest during that time as three of the men he believed to be Confederate guerillas worked themselves into positions where they were close to him. He was alert for any kind of trouble but when the move came it seemed harmless enough.

"Got a question for ye," the man in the buckskin shirt said suddenly. "Name's Cragg, by the way. Ed Cragg. I'm kinda new around here and it seems like I oughta find out whether the place is a good one to git out of."

"Leave," Kimbrell told him shortly, "it's gettin' worse all the time."

"Ye think the war's doin' it?"

"Could be. All I know is the whole territory's goin' loco. Nitwits in uniforms parade around and act important about nothing! Bandits claimin' to be patriotic citizens of somewhere-or-other use the war as an excuse to plunder! Seems like if you give a man a gun nowadays he turns out to be either a damned idiot or a damned thief!"

"Sounds like you don't take much stock in either side," Cragg commented, an edge in his tone although he seemed to be trying hard to sound casual.

"I don't. Politics don't mean a damned thing to me. I don't have any old home state to get sentimental over. The Union is just a name I've heard people use. I think both sides are run by a pack of lunatics. All I want is a chance to make an honest livin' without white men gettin' worse than the Injuns ever dared to be."

Cragg grinned. "You might as well give up hope, friend. There's a war goin' on. You're in it—one way or another."

"Then I'll be in it my way. I'm servin' notice on anybody who cares to listen that I don't give a damn whether a man wears a uniform—or what color uniform he wears. If he makes a move to interfere with my business he's a bandit. I know how to handle bandits."

"You didn't do much about the blue-bellies that brung you in," Cragg pointed out dryly.

"Sure I didn't. For a couple o' mighty good reasons. I was outnumbered and had a hunch they'd be as stupid as they turned out to be. While they was bringin' my train to Pueblo, they kept off the other crooks. A man don't always have to fight to beat his enemies."

"You're calling that militia crowd enemies?"

"For a while I did. Now they're gone and I'm rid of 'em. So I forget about 'em. It's as simple as that."

"That's a hell of a way to talk about men what saved yore Goddam mules!" The words came suddenly and from a little behind Kimbrell.

Before he could even turn to see who was

talking another voice broke in. "Mind ye own damned business! It ain't no skin off'n yore nose even if yo' are a damned Yank."

The two men who now faced each other looked like most of the others in the place, their garb hinting that they might be miners or prospectors rather than farmers. Kimbrell wasn't much interested in that part of it. What caught him by surprise was to realize that he had tabbed both of them as part of Cragg's gang.

At that moment the lantern-jawed youth who had worked in the corral jumped forward to take a wild swing at the man who had spoken first. Two others leaped into the fray and Kimbrell knew what it meant. For some reason a fake fight was being started.

There was a split second for him to recognize his feeling as a warning but no time for him to do anything about it. Somebody—probably Cragg—shoved him right into the brawl and he staggered awkwardly, caught off balance. He grabbed at a flailing arm, but somebody hit him on the back of the head and he went down under the threshing feet. Then everything went black.

Unconsciousness lasted only moments but he couldn't quite get his wits together. Dimly he knew that somebody was going through his pockets but he couldn't make himself do anything about it. All that seemed important was that he should protect his head and face from those heavy boots.

Then his senses came back and he knew that the violence had gone away from him. O'Casey and his war club were taking charge. Men were trampling each other to get out of the door and Kimbrell sat up gingerly, rubbing the knob on the back of his head as he watched the performance. He could even grin painfully as he realized that the men who were taking punishment from the fat Irishman were mere bystanders who had not been involved in the fight. That was the way it always seemed to work out.

"Hold it!" he yelled at O'Casey.

The fat man turned to glower at him. "What the hell!" he exploded. "Ye make me chase my customers away and then ye give me hell fer doin' it!"

Kimbrell struggled to his feet, noting that two of his pockets were still inside out. "Who hit me?" he asked. "The first one, I mean?"

"I didn't see that part. How come it happened?"

Kimbrell pointed to his pockets. "Fake fight. So somebody could search me."

"What'd they git?"

"Nothing. I've been here often enough to know that the only way to come is with empty pockets. After I paid you for that second slug of bad whiskey I didn't have anything at all in my pockets."

"Damn you, you got the best that was in the house!"

"Which was bad enough. How about a wet rag? I'll mop off and get out of here before anything else happens."

"What was the polecats lookin' fer?" the Irishman asked when he had brought a bar rag and helped Kimbrell to clean up a little. "If it was a fake fight they musta been figgerin' on somethin'."

"I wish I knew," Kimbrell told him. "Either they're smarter'n I thought—or dumber. I don't know which."

He was on his mule and heading groggily toward the Ogden stable when a thought came to him. Only one thing could have started that fight. The one thing that several men had seen him put into his pocket was the key to the storeroom where the cartridge boxes were stored.

CHAPTER 9:

No sound broke the stillness of the chilly night when Kimbrell dismounted at the entrance to the Ogden stable. A continuing headache made him abnormally conscious of being cold but worse than the discomfort caused by a wet shirt was the realization that he had made a mess of his evening's venture. Maybe he had accomplished something in the way of establishing himself as an angry neutral but otherwise he had to admit failure. He had been so busy leading up to where he might hope to pick up a hint or two about possible Rebel activities that he had been a sucker for that planned brawl.

He had to assume that someone would follow him to the stable so he did everything that a watcher might expect him to do. He remembered that there was a lantern just inside the door, so he halted there to find it and light it. Then he put the mule into a stall and hung his saddle and bridle on the usual pegs. That gave him a chance to see the key where Pablo had left it in a joint of the door frame—as arranged between them. So far so good.

He forked a bit of extra hay into the two stalls occupied by his mules and blew out the lantern. At the doorway he paused long enough to get the key and transfer it to his pocket. Then he pulled his gun and took a single step into the open, standing there with senses alert for any sign of movement near him.

He waited a full two minutes before moving along the front of the building to the door of the room he planned to occupy. Again he took precautions but once more found no sign of danger. This time he struck no light but simply went out again after making certain that no one was in the place. He was beginning to feel a bit foolish about his own caution when he worked across into the patio-corral and found that the lock was secure on the storeroom. Perhaps he had been wrong about the purpose of that business at O'Casey's.

Still he completed a careful check of the whole area, moving slowly and pausing to listen every few feet. There seemed to be nothing about the place that wasn't quite normal for the small hours of the morning.

He consoled himself that at least he would be able to sleep now, having done everything possible to guard against immediate trouble. But, when he had blocked the door and made sure that there was no easy way of getting through the narrow window, he still found himself wide awake. This attempt to get the key to the storeroom—and he had to assume that the key had been the object of the maneuver—was in the same class with the attacks on the mule train. Somebody wanted them pretty badly. Mere outlaws might well be interested, but Kimbrell couldn't make himself think that the answer was so simple. Mules and cartridges still seemed like the objectives of some sort of military force, a force which persisted in remaining invisible.

He was still awake, puzzling over it, when he heard what sounded like a footfall near the door. He came out of the bunk instantly but without making a sound, picking up his gun as he made the move. He crossed to the door and silently eased away the packing case-chair which blocked it. Then he eased it open and waited again, listening.

"A rat or something," he murmured under his breath. "I'm gettin' jumpy!"

He took a step into the night as the thought went through his mind—and then he didn't think about anything. There was a flash of pain. That was all.

He was cold. It seemed to him that he ought to get up and find an extra blanket but he hated to move because his head ached. Then anger caught at him because it seemed that someone was trying to drag away the blanket he already had. He tried to fight off the thief but found that his hands were being held tight—at the wrists—and he couldn't do anything to help himself.

Then things cleared up a little and he knew that the hands were not bent on blanket larceny at all. Somebody had him by the wrists and was trying to drag him into the room where he had thought he was already sleeping. There was a rosy glow in the sky beyond the trading post so he knew that time had passed. Evidently he was mixed up about a lot of things.

He found strength to twist his arms suddenly, breaking the grip of the person he could not see and taking his own grip on the other pair of wrists. He was almost proud of himself that he did it so swiftly, yanking hard to bring the unknown down across him where he could do battle more efficiently. That was when he got his biggest surprise of all. It was Alice Ogden who came somersaulting out of the stable room to sprawl across his legs.

Kimbrell wasn't sure whether his astonishment was greater than the pain stirred up by his effort. He felt sick—and speechless. Which was perhaps fortunate because he could almost hear himself saying something ridiculous like, "Nice morning, Miss Ogden." Not only would it have been a poor sort of greeting but it wouldn't have been true. It was not a nice morning. It was damned cold!

The girl scrambled clear and started to retreat. Kimbrell fought off the hazy foolishness and opened his eyes. "Sorry," he mumbled, the words coming with an effort. "I guess I didn't know—"

She stopped, staring at him with open distaste. “You’re drunk!”

He still had that crazy urge to say something foolish. “Drunk with knobs on my skull! Want to feel ’em?”

“Now I’m sure you’re drunk! And I was trying to help you because I thought you’d been hurt!”

The shivers caught him again, keeping him from going on with the idiocy. He struggled to get his numbed legs under him, wondering whether they would hold him. By using the door frame he managed to pull himself erect before running cautious fingers through his hair. There was a second sore place now to keep company with the first one. “Sorry,” he said finally. “I guess I sound drunk, all right. But I’m not. When did you find me here?”

“Only a few minutes ago. Are you really injured?”

“I reckon I’ll live—but I’m not feeling real spry. Two knocks on even a thick head don’t help a man much.”

“You mean you were attacked?”

“Right. Want to come inside? I’m cold.”

He didn’t expect her to accept the invitation but she did. When he almost fell in trying to pick up the overturned chair so that he could slump into it she came quickly to his aid. After that her moves were swift and efficient. She put a wet cloth on the back of his head, threw a blanket around his shoulders and started a fire in the stove. For a girl who had obviously been reared in softer surroundings she seemed to know what she was about.

If she had any curiosity about his misfortunes she didn't ask questions. It was Kimbrell who pulled himself together enough to ask, "How'd you happen to find me at this hour of the morning?"

"Quite simple. I was worried about that ammunition you locked up in the little warehouse. At the first break of dawn I decided to see that nothing had happened out there. I think I dreamed that someone broke in. Or maybe I simply thought about it because I feared something like that would happen."

"Find anything wrong?"

"Very much wrong. The boxes are gone. The door was wide open and the key is still sticking in the padlock."

He told her of what had happened at O'Casey's place and added his theory that the effort had been made because somebody wanted the key. Then he lied a little. "The key was still here in the stable but I made the mistake of putting it back into my pocket when I was ready to turn in for the night. After that I got stupid. I heard a noise and went out to look around. Somebody caught me from behind and knocked me out—real good. Then they took the key and stole the cartridges."

She studied him frankly, trouble showing in little lines around her dark eyes. Then she asked, "Do you feel all right now? You talk sanely enough—but your eyes don't seem to be quite right. Are you having dizzy spells or something?"

"I'm doing fine," he assured her. "You're just confused at seeing me with a clean face." He rubbed the fresh stubble on his chin and changed the remark to, ". . . with almost a clean face."

She laughed briefly then. "I guess you're all right—and I noticed the difference when I first found you lying in the doorway. At first I did not realize that it was you."

"I hope you think it's some improvement?" The words seemed to come out without his having formed them.

She smiled again. "No doubt about it. Also no doubt about your being better. Speeches like that are the routine male performance. So you're normal again. Your eyes looked so odd that it had me worried."

Having done well with the first attempt, he tried again. "I'm flattered that you should be worried. But I'll let you in on a secret. My eyes fool a lot of people." He went on to explain how many people had told him of the effect produced by the unconscious trick of being wide-eyed when most folks tended to squint a little. "I was trying to get my wits together—so my eyes came wide open, I suppose. Don't worry about it. Maybe you'd better worry about the puzzle. You folks could be more concerned by it than I am. You've got more to lose."

He wasn't sure how he'd gotten himself into that bit of hot water but there was no point in trying to unsay what he had said. He needed to confide in someone and Alice Ogden seemed like his best bet. Maybe he was thinking that way because she was a very pretty girl, but he still felt that there was more to his decision than mere impulse. Anyway, he didn't propose to explain his own status as an agent of Colonel St. Vrain and he wouldn't mention the fact that the stolen cartridge boxes had contained no cartridges.

"It's this business of there being a Confederate force in the territory," he said. "I don't seem to have much success in getting anybody to believe that there is such a force. You heard the talk yesterday. Everybody thinks I'm dreaming it up—but my idea is that we can't afford to assume that it's not around somewhere."

"Why don't you come to breakfast with us," she said, the smile coming again, "and go over this with Father. He may be able to stir up Governor Gilpin and have some search made for this mysterious force."

Kimbrell shook his head. "I don't think your father is the one to do the job."

"Why not?" The smile was gone and the warmth had left her tone.

Kimbrell hesitated. He could sense that what he was going to say was not going to be very palatable to her. Anyhow, he didn't quite know how to say it. "He's too blunt," he managed finally. "If he gets a hint that anything disloyal is taking place around here he'll be calling all Southern sympathizers damned traitors."

"Aren't they?" Now the tone was really sharp.

"No. They're not. Most of them side with the South for the same reason that you side with the North. That's the way you were brought up. The whole thing is that the idea of patriotism doesn't mean the same thing to all people."

"And you are an authority on that subject, I suppose?"

He ignored the challenge, trying to make her understand. "Likely I know less about it than most people. Or maybe I can see both sides because I don't have any reason to feel blind loyalty to either side. I can feel mighty disgusted with the two sets of bullheaded idiots who started it in the first place. If the leaders had been locked up two years ago, we wouldn't have any war."

"That's ridiculous! So why are you taking sides with the Union if you don't think the cause is just."

"Because I'm not making any judgments about just causes. I favor the Union for purely selfish reasons. I'm a business man—like your father—"

She turned toward the door. "Please forget the breakfast invitation. I'm sure that it would be a mistake for you to talk to Father."

"One thing. I spoke to you in confidence. I'd appreciate it if you'd keep it that way."

"Why should I?"

"Get ready to be mad at me again. You won't like this but I don't want your father stirring up the kind of fuss which I can imagine him stirring. To him everything is cut and dried. Good is good. Right is right. Wrong is wrong. Anybody who is not a staunch Unionist is a traitor. In this part of the country that's simply not true. A lot of people from Southern states don't approve of the war but this thing called patriotism makes them feel a sympathy toward old homes and old neighbors. Right now they're keeping pretty quiet but it wouldn't take much to move them. I don't want to see any more men moving into Confederate ranks. Hot talk could do it."

"I shall respect your confidence," she told him icily. "I'm sure I would not care to give circulation to ideas as preposterous as yours!" Then she went out.

For several minutes Kimbrell sat there and let the ache in his head pound away. Maybe he deserved it. It didn't seem that he had done anything right so far. The minor success of his strategy in getting the enemy to steal a couple of worthless boxes could not offset the fact that he had failed completely in his effort to alert Coloradans to the danger which he believed faced them. Somehow he had to find evidence that they would believe.

CHAPTER 10:

At first he had considered telling Alice about being an agent for St. Vrain, but before he reached the trading post he decided against it. There was no point in stirring up any more fuss. His job now was to get word to St. Vrain—and to protect his own interests by heading south. His ruse had taken the immediate enemy to the west where they couldn't do any damage to the wagon train but they would soon discover that they had been tricked. Somebody would see through the strategy, of course. Maybe he had actually prodded them into making an attempt against the wagons since now they would suspect that he had a big reason for keeping them away. It wasn't a cheerful thought. Even when he made a small success it threatened to cause more trouble.

Getting out of town without giving anybody ideas was simple enough. He headed east through the settlement, stopping twice to ask about Colonel Boone's present whereabouts and learning that the Indian Agent was at Fort Wise. That would let people think that he was on his way down the river. He took the river trail far enough to let him make certain that he was not being followed and then he made his crossing, heading south toward the north approach to

Raton Pass. It was not a regular trail but it would let him avoid the scattered ranches which had sprung up along the Arkansas.

He didn't travel very far. By mid-afternoon his head was aching worse and lack of sleep was making him feel groggy. So he made a dry camp along what was a creek at some seasons. There was some risk in using such scant cover but he decided to take the chance. Probably he did not need to worry over enemy activity for at least another day or two. By that time he would need to be ready. Getting some rest was pretty important.

A good night's sleep made him feel better and he rode on south in a better frame of mind. A little after noon he cut the main trail between Pueblo and Raton Pass—and his spirits took a sharp drop. Fresh sign told him that five men had moved south along the trail. His own party had numbered only four.

It was just about an hour later that the sign told him something else. He found other sets of hoofmarks, this time four of them. Four riders had gone down the trail from this point, probably only hours ahead of the other five. He guessed that Esteban and the others had avoided the trail until they were well away from Pueblo but then had picked it up. The others had been only a little behind them, perhaps even keeping them in sight. Either the muleskinners hadn't been as clever as they had hoped in getting out of Pueblo or the enemy had been lucky. The latter guess seemed most likely. Probably Cragg—or whoever was giving the orders—had sent a scout detail out to watch for the wagon train while the rest of the gang stole the cartridges. Or maybe the truth was a variation of that guess. Possibly some able-bodied men had been left with the wounded at the ranch—which Kimbrell had carefully skirted early that morning. Cragg could have sent a messenger for men at that point to take over the scout duty.

"Stop guessing, Sam!" he told himself aloud. There were times when a man had to make guesses but now was not one of them. He had to deal with a fact. Five supposed enemies were between himself and his men.

He studied the tracks constantly as he rode, seeing no indication that the five men had shown any excitement at seeing the other tracks angling in from the northwest. Maybe they knew about the Kimbrell party. Maybe they expected other members of their own crowd to join them. Kimbrell was guessing again.

Again he made an early camp. His enemies would be moving cautiously and probably would hide any fire they might make. He couldn't afford to reveal himself yet. The only sensible course was to stick to saddlebag rations and stay out of sight. Another day might tell him more about the situation ahead. There didn't seem to be any emergency. He had figured things out pretty carefully and estimated that Esteban and the others were perhaps fourteen hours ahead of him, twelve on the time of departure from Pueblo and another two he had lost in catching up on his rest. The other party were about midway between himself and his men, give or take a couple of hours either way. While it remained like that he could play safe and try to get back a little more energy.

Two hours' ride next morning showed him the still warm ashes of a tiny fire which had been built between high rocks. So the enemy party was two hours ahead of him. Somehow that pleased him a little. He preferred to have it that way rather than to know that they were closing in on the rear of his own men. Not that he needed to fear Esteban being surprised. The wily New Mexican would be keeping a keen eye on his own backtrail. Maybe he already knew that somebody was behind him.

The next day—after losing nearly five hours in flat country where the sign told him of some sort of shoe trouble with his party's third horse—he began to work into the first easy approaches of the Ratons. He knew that the other party was holding its interval behind Esteban's men. They had not tried to overtake the New Mexicans when the halt was made but instead had done some loafing as though not wanting to get closer. So they were not casual travelers and they were not trying to catch men whose horses were loaded with ammunition. It was a scout party.

Just before dusk he found that the five men whose trail he had been studying seemed to lose interest in the trail itself. They had turned off into a wooded canyon where the foothills began to turn into real mountains. They had ridden single file into the dark recesses of a gorge which dropped away to a lower level while the trail itself went into a steep climb.

Kimbrell knew better than to believe that they had decided not to follow his men. This particular gorge was actually an alternate trail but one which could not be used by wagons. Riders occasionally used it to save a little distance but the grade at the far end was impossible even for pack mules. He had never been across it but he recalled that Esteban had once pointed out a hogback which marked the spot where the crooked passage began its final climb to join the main trail. It seemed likely that these men would use that hogback as a lookout point. From that spot they would be able to see the wagons when they started down the long winding grade. They would be able to estimate manpower and make proper plans for their attack. Then, returning across the shortcut, they could meet the rest of their gang and set up their ambush. Kimbrell didn't waste time doubting that others would arrive to lend a hand or that an ambush was intended.

He calculated his chances carefully, mindful of the fact that the air was taking on a raw chill which promised an uncomfortable night. To ride on up the main trail would be a risky business but it seemed like the only course open to him. He had to meet those wagons and warn his men. To remain here and perhaps be trapped between two lots of enemies didn't make any sense at all. He didn't have any choice.

It was darkening rapidly when he started his tired horse up the tortuous trail which had seen the wreckage of so many wagons. Speed was not important now so he moved with all possible caution, knowing that the big thing was to get past those men in the lower gorge without being detected. One thing in his favor was that the cold was coming on the wings of a brisk northwest wind. Even the sound of an iron hoof on rock would not carry far tonight. Things were working out in his favor for a change.

The journey became a matter of fighting fatigue and drowsiness as well as keeping warm. Then the horse began to show signs of wearing out and he kept warm without any trouble at all, sweating a little as he had to practically drag the animal through some of the worst stretches. In the darkness of an overcast night he could not see the trail itself so he had no chance to judge his own speed or distance. He simply kept going until he felt certain that he had passed the upper junction of the trails. Then he groped his way into some thick timber and halted for the night.

CHAPTER 11:

A spit of wet snow in his face woke him while it was still dark. Partly because he was too cold to sleep again he saddled the horse and began more of that cautious groping along the trail. It seemed like a smart precaution even though he couldn't exactly enjoy it. In case the snow put a blanket on the trail he would not be leaving tell-tale tracks so close to where the enemy scouts were waiting.

Dawn came about an hour later and with it an end to the light snow. He found sign as soon as the flakes began to disappear from the ground and knew that he had actually by-passed the enemy scouts. Only four men had ridden the trail ahead of him. Maybe his guesses were getting better.

Noon had passed and he was feeling the pangs of hunger when he found the wagons. Men were toiling to clear a section of the pass where a rock slide had completely blocked the trail. He could see that they had been at the task for quite a long time, perhaps as much as three or four days.

Emilio Vasquez rode forward to meet him as soon as one of the workmen passed the word about his approach. Vasquez looked as trim and dandified as usual, but that was no surprise to Kimbrell. The lean New Mexican always looked that way even in circumstances worse than the present ones. It was amazing that he could lend a hand with manual labor, oversee workmen, fight Indians or carouse with drunken muleskinners but still come out of it looking as though he had never been out of the reception room of the Governor's Palace.

The two men wasted no time in greetings but got right down to business. Vasquez reported simply—but in rather elegant Spanish—that there had been no attempts at interference with the train, either by Indians or by guerilla bands. The early delays had been incidental to normal business but in the pass they had encountered a great deal of storm damage to the trail. He had begun to worry about early snows even before Esteban and the others arrived to let him know that human trouble was ahead.

Kimbrell filled in the things which Esteban had not been able to report, realizing that the dapper New Mexican was expecting him to take charge. That was one of the reasons why their partnership had worked out so well. Vasquez had always been the business man at the Santa Fe end. Anything connected with the actual movement of freight was Kimbrell's sole responsibility. Although Vasquez was nominal commander of the militia company which was also the freighting crew, it would still be Kimbrell who would have to make decisions.

"When did Esteban arrive?" Kimbrell asked as they started toward the stalled train.

"Early yesterday."

"Then he will be well rested. I want scouts out ahead of us. Esteban and Pablo, I think."

Vasquez smiled, showing strong white teeth beneath the carefully trimmed mustache. "You will give the orders?"

"Just on this matter. Only to Esteban and Pablo. This is war. The enemy ahead is part of the Confederate army—in some fashion or other. Our men are Union troops. I am a civilian. You will have to keep that in mind."

They worked their way across the rock slide, passing the workmen who were digging a passage through it. Kimbrell exchanged banter with some of the men, noting that a cook wagon had been moved up with the work crews so that they could eat in shifts. Vasquez had been using his head.

They halted where off-duty crewmen were eating and he saw that El Toro had pitched in as cook's helper. Pablo was with the off-duty gang, evidently about finished with his meal. Kimbrell went directly to the youngster.

"Finish eating," he instructed the lad. "Then find Esteban and bring him here. Both of you come ready to ride. Carry revolvers but no other guns."

"Pedro also, señor?"

"No. Just you and Esteban. I'll want Pedro with me."

He turned to face the other men then, explaining exactly what danger was ahead of them. "I think we will be able to move by tomorrow—if all of you work hard to roll the boulders away. The rest of the pass is clear except for the enemy soldiers who will try to stop us. Esteban and Pablo will have told us by that time of the enemy plans. Then we will make our own plans as to how we shall defeat them. Captain Vasquez will give you the proper orders when the time comes."

He sat down with them to eat after that, using the time to get more information from Vasquez. New Mexico was full of rumors, some of them almost certainly true. A large force of Texans was supposed to be on the Pecos but no one of any repute had seen them. On the other hand there was plenty of reason to believe that a sizeable army was actually on the upper Rio Grande. Colonel Sibley was undoubtedly planning a big invasion. Fort Union was practically in a state of panic, undermanned and vulnerable.

"Get a man picked out for a messenger job," Kimbrell said briefly. "We won't send him until after we see what happens in the lower pass, but then he can take word to Colonel St. Vrain. I don't know what he can do about convincing those thickheads to the north but I sure as hell want him to know that there's plenty of reason to try."

He slept after that, waking to find that it was

night again. Esteban and Pablo had not returned but they appeared just as he was finishing a quick supper. They had had just enough daylight for their Indian act, getting close enough to the men in the lower ravine to overhear some of the talk. The ambush plan was just as Kimbrell had guessed it to be. Cragg and a strong force of Confederate irregulars would arrive at the lower end of the pass not later than the next morning. They would wait there until the scouts in the lower gorge rode down to warn them that the wagons were coming.

"It is not to be an ambush," Esteban declared. "It is to be a massacre. They will count the wagons and kill all but enough wagoners to drive the teams which they do not have men to handle. There is to be no quarter given. That much I heard clearly enough."

"Did you hear any names? Madison, for example?"

"Cragg is their leader. They do this without knowledge of Madison. They say that Madison would not approve of their plans. I do not think they approve much of Madison."

"Not bloodthirsty enough to suit 'em, I reckon. I suppose you've got a plan all ready for giving them a dose of their own medicine?"

Esteban grinned. "It is possible," he admitted modestly.

"Where do you figure they'll make their try?"

"Where the two trails come together down the mountain."

"I kinda thought that would be the place. It's smart. They want to let our men get the wagons over the worst places before they take over—from dead men. Let's go talk to Vasquez. I want him to know just how we're thinking and what we plan to do about it." He made it sound easy but that wasn't the way he felt. War was being used as an excuse for outright murder.

They worked over the plans in considerable detail and it was late when Kimbrell crawled into his blankets again. Tonight he would try to catch up on his rest and get the last aches out of his head. Before long he would need every faculty he could muster.

The next morning he held rifle drill as the first order of business. Only when he was satisfied did he let the men get on with breakfast. Then the teams were spanned in and wagons began the long downgrade.

Kimbrell rode with a teamster on the third wagon, having other men who might normally have acted as flankers do the same. If the enemy had a sentry out he wanted them to see a train which seemed unguarded. They kept to that arrangement until they had passed the spot where he knew enemy eyes would be watching. He had seen nothing on the lower level as they passed but he hadn't expected to. The watchers would keep well hidden.

He let the last wagon pull well clear of the open stretch and then signaled the halt. Almost as he did so Pablo came up out of the brush on the lower slope, grinning excitedly as he reported what had happened down in the gorge. He and his companions had circled the lookout party and had seen about a dozen men setting up their ambush exactly as predicted. They obviously planned to open fire just as the lead wagons came down the last steep pitch.

He had left Esteban and Pedro at that point and had doubled back to watch the sentries. He had seen them take cover to count the wagons that were passing above them. Then they had moved down the gorge to join the others at the ambush scene. There would be close to twenty men in the ambush party. It appeared that they would be divided, about half of them on each side of the main trail so as to bewilder their victims with a crossfire.

Kimbrell waved to the six men he had selected to join him, the men who had shown the most familiarity with the new carbines. He would have to take a chance on their marksmanship. "Start the teams," he told Vasquez.

"We'll be there long before the wagons can get down the mountain. Make sure that every man knows he's to take cover at the first sound of a gun. We'll fire it, I promise, so the drivers don't need to worry about getting hit by surprise fire." He changed his tone a little, remembering that he was talking to the officer who was the actual military commander. "I'd suggest, Captain, that you post your best marksmen on the right-hand side—facing the upper slope. We'll try to handle the ambushers on the left. Does that sound all right to you?"

Vasquez smiled. "I shall give the proper orders," he said briefly. "Take care."

They left their horses with the wagons, moving out in single file behind Pablo who claimed that he had found a short way to the gorge. It was shorter, no doubt, but it was rough and steep. Kimbrell dropped back to the rear, mainly so that he could inspect each man's weapon and make certain that no one was sliding along over the rocks with a cocked gun. It was no time for having accidents.

They found the gorge trail without difficulty and five minutes later were facing Esteban. Pedro was on watch behind the ambushers, the squatty man reported. Everything was going just as they had understood it. About half of the guerillas had climbed to sniping points above the lower fork of the trail and the balance were to strike from the angle itself. The orders had been given. The first eight drivers were to be killed at the opening fire. The others could be taken prisoner later and forced to drive wagons for the captors.

"Where are the enemy's horses?" Kimbrell asked.

Esteban gestured vaguely to the north. "Farther down," he said. "I have not seen them. I think they try to keep them out of the line of fire."

"Let me take a look at the place," Kimbrell said. "Maybe we'll have a try at the horses. Maybe we won't. This is the important matter, right here."

He motioned for the rest of his party to hold their positions, then he followed Esteban cautiously down the easy slope of the gorge bottom. Pedro backed out of a pine thicket to raise a warning finger, pointing back through the pines. There was a whispered conference and again Kimbrell was assured that the enemy plans were quite clear and as reported. The three of them crawled forward perhaps a hundred feet, mostly having it easy because they could use a carpet of pine needles to muffle their movements. Presently Kimbrell could see the edge of the main trail. Well above it two men were in plain sight, evidently on the lookout and ready to conceal themselves at the first sign of the wagon train. Closer at hand four patches of brown or gray indicated the positions of the bushwhackers who were posted below the trail.

He grunted his understanding and began to back out. The enemy had made a good choice of position for the ambush—but he had completely neglected his rear. The opportunity for a hard smash was too good to miss.

"We'll take them just before the train gets into the danger spot," he told his men when they were together again. "I want to take prisoners, if possible. Maybe we can make somebody talk. None of you is to fire a shot until I do. I'll try to bluff them into surrender but I won't hold back long if the bluff fails to work. If I fire—you get going fast. Have a target picked out and be ready. Understood?"

They spread out to begin the crawl through the pines which filled the angle between the trails. Esteban at one end of the line and Pablo at the other were to serve as guides. Kimbrell set the pace in the middle, his mind beginning to wrestle with the problem of timing. He wanted to let the wagons get into position so that the men on them could lend a hand in any fight which broke out, but he didn't dare hold back too long. He regretted that he had not given some more specific orders about going for the enemy's horses but now it was too late. His men were trying hard to move in complete silence through the pines and he couldn't risk having them passing orders along.

They were almost at the point where he had made his quick observation when he heard the distant grate and clink of wagons coming down that last steep pitch. He knew that this would be the slow part of the move. One wagon would make the descent under firm braking before a second would risk starting. That part he would have to watch with due care, remembering what his scouts had told him about the enemy plans. He couldn't let them have their chosen targets in front of them before he was ready to make his own move.

Then he knew that there would be ample time, perhaps too much. Already he could see two crouching figures ahead of him. Two men in rough garb were staring up at the main trail, rifles already pointed.

He knew that others of his men had seen enemy troops. The clear click of guns being cocked reached his ears and he wondered why the sound had not altered the enemy. Still he didn't dare pass along any word of caution. His men were already too close to the enemy for any extra sound to be made.

Suddenly he heard a man growl, "Dammit! There's somebody movin' back in the pines. Which one o' these fine sojers o' ours has snuck out on us?"

Cragg's voice came clearly in reply. "Check the line, Lem. I'll kill any man who turns coward! Hey!"

The final exclamation was enough for Kimbrell. He couldn't wait to find out what had caused it. He practically broke in on the sound itself as he shouted, “Throw down your guns and stand up! You’re covered.”

The one swift reaction within his range of vision was that one of the crouching men whirled to aim his rifle at the sound of the challenge. Kimbrell had no choice. His orders would keep his men from defending themselves unless he fired first. That couldn’t happen. He fired before the rifleman could get into decent aiming position, knocking the man down with the first slug. Then he tried again.

“Hold it, I tell you! That’s a sample of what happens to any man who resists. Come out of there with your hands up!”

It surprised him that no other firing came to interrupt the words. There was even a short silence when he was finished. Then Cragg shouted, “Who’s talkin’?”

Kimbrell could see that another man was trying to get into position to screen himself from this threat from his rear. He wasn’t having too much success.

“Just throw down your guns!” Kimbrell shouted.

This time Cragg’s defiance was prompt. “It’s a bluff, men!” he shouted. “They’re in the pines. Just them four. Git ’em!”

Kimbrell could see enough to know that his men were obeying orders. Three of them were trying to claw a way into the pines directly in front of him. The fight was on.

CHAPTER 12:

Guns began to bang all along the line. Kimbrell saw one of the charging ambushers go down and he yelled another order. “Don’t let ’em get to their horses!” The yell drew the attention of the second attacker and Kimbrell had to move fast to knock the fellow over before he could steady himself to fire. Still there was time for him to wonder whether his order had been heard above the din. In the excitement it didn’t occur to him that he had shouted in English and that none of the nearer teamsters would have understood.

A slug threw dirt at his feet and more crashed through the pines above him. Apparently others of the enemy were shooting at the sound of his voice. He scrambled quickly to another opening and then he saw Cragg moving toward him, firing a revolver as he came. There was a split second for him to wonder at the brand-new gray campaign hat that the other man was wearing and then he was getting his gun around. Both men fired at the same moment and Cragg went down.

Kimbrell came to his feet then, running forward as yells of panic told him that the enemy had gone into full retreat. “Cut ’em off!” he yelled lustily. “Don’t let them get away.”

The order was too late. Already three of the

ambushers were headed down into the fork of the trail, only Esteban making any attempt to fire at them.

Kimbrell didn't have time to do a thing about it. More distant shots caught his attention and he saw that the other half of the ambush party had moved to take a hand. Men were coming down the mountain from their hiding places to support retreating comrades. Again Kimbrell shouted orders, this time remembering to put them into Spanish. "Take cover! Look out for the men above the trail!"

He could see that the second wave had decided to ignore the wagons in order to get at the unknowns who had started the fight below the trail. Things were going to get a mite mixed-up among the pines with some of the first lot of enemies still full of fight.

That was when Vasquez demonstrated that he wasn't as soft as he looked. Somehow he had sized up the situation and gathered a half dozen of his nearest men. They were charging straight down the trail, Vasquez on horseback and his men straggling out behind him. Apparently the ambushers on the upper slope didn't see him until they were beginning to cross the trail itself. They had been firing down the mountain side in their effort to support their fellows and now they found themselves taking a hard flank attack. Wagoners halted to take steady aim, letting their captain dash in to empty his revolver and gallop straight on through the enemy. It was more than a little foolhardy on Vasquez's part but it worked. Some of the enemy went down and the others broke for cover. In a matter of minutes the fight was over but Kimbrell could feel a little disgruntled about the results. The wagons had been well defended but at least half of the enemy force had made good its escape. He could hear horses pounding away down the lower trail. They would carry the word back—which was what he had hoped could be avoided.

"Take charge here," he called to Pedro as the young fellow swung toward him with a happy grin on his face. "Make sure you flush out anybody who's hiding. And don't take any risks if you can help it."

He climbed quickly to the trail where Vasquez was getting his men into position for a possible counter-attack. There were three enemy dead on or near the trail and Vasquez looked quite proud of himself.

Kimbrell remembered the military formalities so he reported briskly, "I think we did it, Captain. Thanks to your prompt action up here. It's too bad we didn't bag the whole gang but they'll think twice before they tackle our boys again."

After that came the dirty business of mop-up. None of the Vasquez men had suffered even a scratch but the vicious fighting in the pines had been a different matter. Two of Kimbrell's party had been killed and another was nursing a long furrow on his shoulder. The dead men had been good drivers and loyal employees. Kimbrell would have taken pains to give them proper burial in any event but now he knew that a morale factor was involved. The Third New Mexico Scouts had had its baptism of fire. They could feel that they were really soldiers. Their casualties should receive due military honors.

By the time the last of the wagons had made the descent to the easier trail below the fork most of the arrangements had been made and the battlefield was cleared. Vasquez—after some earnest talk with Kimbrell—assumed the duty of handling the burial ceremony, doing a remarkably good job of improvising a burial service. Kimbrell's private opinion was that the man would have made a good priest but he was careful not to say so. This was important to the men and Vasquez understood the importance of what he was doing.

They were less ceremonious with the enemy casualties. Eight dead men—and Kimbrell didn't ask any awkward questions about the absence of wounded, knowing how New Mexicans felt about the hated "Texans"—posed something of a problem. Esteban solved it quickly enough. He had noticed a little ravine at the far side of the lower gorge so they put the bodies there, covering them with rocks and dirt. Undoubtedly Esteban and some of the others knew that among the dead there were farm boys whom they had known along the Arkansas but they said nothing about it. Better to let the impression continue that the enemies were all Texans. New Mexicans would feel better about it.

Kimbrell forced himself to the grisly task of searching each body before turning it over to the burial detail. He had hoped to find something which he might send to Denver as evidence of a large Confederate force in the territory but the search produced only the loose coins, tobacco, knives and other personal items that such men would be carrying. Cragg's body was no real exception. The man had carried nearly fifty dollars in gold and notes but there was nothing on him to satisfy Kimbrell's hopes.

"There is the evidence of the hat," Vasquez pointed out, his voice so steady that Kimbrell knew that it was a matter of stern effort. "Such hats are issued only to Confederate officers, I believe."

"We'll keep it," Kimbrell agreed. "Maybe it'll shake somebody up."

"Better to take it for yourself," Esteban suggested with one of his ugly grins. "Your own is not so good."

Kimbrell grimaced. That brawl on O'Casey's floor had left its marks. "I'm kinda partial to this hat," he said. "Twice I got banged on the head while I was wearing it. The hat took some of the sting. Honorable wounds, you might call the marks."

"Look at it," Vasquez advised dryly.

Kimbrell removed the battered headgear and stared. "So that's where Cragg's slug went! He sure as hell didn't miss by much." The crown of the hat had been sliced wide open.

"So you need a new hat," Esteban grinned.

Kimbrell did not reply. He didn't like the idea of trying on the hat of a man he had just killed but he didn't want to show any such feeling before the men. After he had played his hand so carefully to make themselves recognize themselves as a military unit he couldn't afford to look silly.

He tried it on gingerly and took it off again. "A bit too small," he said with some relief. "Anyway, it's still valuable evidence. I hope." Then he noticed that there was quite a bulge in the sweat band. Evidently Cragg had not been supplied with a hat that actually fitted him and he had made it smaller.

Kimbrell ran his fingers behind the leather and brought out a folded strip of newspaper. "Hello!" he exclaimed. "Maybe we've really got some evidence! If this is a Texas paper—"

He broke off abruptly as he saw that the news print was from the bottom of a sheet, bearing no date line. The important part was that folded into the newspaper was another sheet with writing on it.

"I think you have really found something, amigo," Vasquez commented in the same quiet tone he generally used.

Kimbrell scanned it hastily. "You're damned right. This oughta convince somebody." He read it aloud, translating sentence for sentence so that all of his listeners would understand. It had all been done in longhand, perhaps hastily, but somebody had tried to make it sound quite official.

> "The Sovereign State of Texas, putting special faith and confidence in Edward Elmer Cragg does hereby commission him as a lieutenant in the armed forces of the said sovereign state. He will act under proper orders issued by superior officers duly commissioned by the State of Texas or by the Confederate States of America. All persons owing loyalty to the State of Texas or to the Confederate States of America will take due notice and acknowledge his authority to act for either of the aforementioned governments.
>
> "This commission is issued by the undersigned in pursuance of authority delegated for that purpose."

The signature was George Madison, Captain, C.S.A.

Kimbrell hesitated a moment or two after completing the reading and translation. Then he looked up at Vasquez. "Captain," he said formally. "Would you be so good as to supply me with a dependable messenger? I think we should get word of this to Colonel St. Vrain." After that he added, "How we manage about letting Denver know is something else. I've got a hunch we'd better work through the commander at Fort Wise. He might understand better."

He was trying to hit on a good plan while the crew worked the wagons down the trail where they could be reorganized into a proper train once more. This still was not evidence that a large Confederate force existed in the territory. Cragg might well have been given a commission as a sort of blind or perhaps merely to organize guerilla forces. Some of the bandit leaders in Missouri were reputed to have Confederate commission. Maybe the same device was being tried in Colorado.

The train was about ready to move on in routine formation when a young New Mexican hurried down the slope as fast as his feet would carry him. He was so breathless that it took a little while to get his meaning, but Kimbrell knew at once that something had gone wrong at the rear. This lad and three others had been herding extra stock along and had fallen well behind the wagons. Apparently they had taken pains to make certain that they didn't close the gap until they were sure that all of the fighting was over.

Kimbrell didn't wait for the boy to become completely coherent. He motioned to several of the men who were about to mount mules and act as guards for the wagons. Esteban and one of the Ortiz twins saw what was happening and promptly claimed horses or mules for themselves and for Kimbrell. It suited the tall man well enough to note that most of his volunteer force was made up of men who had sided him in the gorge. He felt that he could depend on them after that other fight.

They went up the steep trail at a dead run, prodding their mounts hard. Before they reached the top of the first climb, however, Esteban uttered a shout of disgust. Just beyond the halted stock they could see that two of the guards were holding their guns on a single rider—who did not appear to be particularly concerned over what had happened to him. The stranger was tall, rather gangling, and his lack of worry was indicated by the way he sat his pony with one lean leg curled around the horn of his saddle. There was a revolver in a holster at his right hip but he had evidently made no attempt to use it, preferring to sit and wait until someone came along to rid him of the pests who were aiming their guns at him. His disdain was clear even at a distance.

Kimbrell had a hunch. He was still holding the gray hat in one hand, not having found any place to put it when he had mounted so hurriedly. Now he stuck it on his head, ramming his own battered hat into a saddlebag. "Let me do the talking," he warned Esteban in a low tone. "Line your men up and look military. I've got a funny feeling about this hombre."

The lounging stranger lost some of his air of boredom as he watched Kimbrell's approach. "Right natty lookin' lot o' Mexes yo' got theah, friend," he drawled. "What the hell kind o' guns are they totin'? I nevah seen none like 'em."

"I'll ask the questions!" Kimbrell snapped. "Who are you and what's your business?"

The lanky man started to protest about unfriendly treatment but Kimbrell broke in, sensing that the fellow was putting on an act. Without turning his head he ordered, "Sergeant Mendoza! Come up here and search this man. Take his gun first." Kimbrell's weapon was out as he spoke, warning the other against trying resistance.

The search was thorough but fruitless. There was nothing on the man's person or in his gear to indicate who he was or what his errand might be. When it was over he aimed a grin at Kimbrell, keen eyes belying the grin. "Yo' got any authority to do this searchin', friend? Anything besides that gun, I mean?"

"Maybe the gun's enough. And these other guns. Did you come up here from Santa Fe or Fort Union? Better answer if you know what's good for you."

"Any reason why it's gotta be either one?"

"No. But it seems likely. Damned Yank posts keep sendin' couriers all the time. I kinda like keepin' track o' what the bastards is worryin' about."

"Sounds like yo' ain't real fond o' Yanks."

Kimbrell shook his head. "I ain't. But it's nothin' real personal with me like it is with a lot of our boys. I'll even offer you a fair deal. You tell me what kind of word you're carryin' and I'll turn you loose. Nobody will know where I got the tale you give me." He hoped he was sounding properly treacherous.

The lean man shook his head. "I'm not a messenger from any forts. You got me wrong."

"Better think about it, mister. We're honest Confederate troops, not outlaws, but these boys o' mine still like to handle things the way they learned to do when they was fightin' Injuns. They git real rough when they need to make a man talk."

"Confederate troops, eh? Anything to prove it?"

"I got a commission. Wrote down and all proper."

"Who signed it?"

"Cap'n Madison. Who else?" Kimbrell had to hope that he wasn't talking to the real Captain George Madison. At first he had been playing a wild hunch but quickly had decided that there were real possibilities in what he was trying to do.

The other man seemed impressed. "A real Madison paper, eh? That's kinda important—if yo' ain't lyin' to me."

"A paper—and a hat," Kimbrell told him proudly, beginning to build up the character he had suddenly decided to be. "I'll even show you."

He dug the paper out of his pocket and announced, still with that careful note of pride, "That's me. Edward Elmer Cragg. You can forget about the Elmer part. I never did like that name."

The lanky man scanned the paper and handed it back. "Looks like yo're jest what yo' claim, friend. Seems kinda like ole times to be seein' Madison's name on a paper. Is the ole rascal still wearin' that fancy goatee he useta sport?"

Kimbrell almost nodded in spite of his wariness. The question had come out so innocently that it had almost trapped him. "Hell, mister," he growled, "I ain't never seen this damned Madison. Colonel Heffiner tells him who's supposed to get these commissions and he writes 'em out. I got mine because I get along real good with Mexes. Mostly they don't like Texans so Madison can't git nowhere with 'em. Him and me kinda operate different parts of the deal." He was practically amazed at himself as the explanation seemed to build up as it went along. Maybe he was a better liar than he had ever realized.

The lanky man seemed impressed. "My business is with Madison," he confided. "Where do I find him?"

"I dunno. We just gobbled up a wagon outfit that was headed north. Likely he's show up when he gits the word but then again mebbe he won't. Damned if I'm goin' to worry about it. I'll have plenty trouble gettin' them wagons back into the mountains without somebody raisin' hell." He let his amiable tone fade away as he added, "That's one reason why I ain't keen on havin' no strangers around. I reckon we'll jest have to keep you fer a pet. Tied up!"

"Wait a bit," the lanky man interrupted, his laziness no longer showing. "I think we can understand each other. Names don't mean a thing and I don't carry papers in my business but maybe this will straighten things out a mite. The name's Ober. Clate Ober." He was dragging at his cartridge belt as he spoke, spreading the overlap of leather near the buckle. The action opened a small slit and from the opening he carefully worked out a thin brass plate about two inches long by an inch and a quarter wide. His grin was confident as he held it out for Kimbrell's inspection.

Kimbrell took a good look. In the center of the plate were etched a pair of crossed pistols. Across the bottom was the word Texas. In the three angles formed by the pistols at top and sides were the letters C.S.A. Kimbrell understood that he was looking at some sort of private identification device. At first he thought of simply taking it and making the man a prisoner but then he decided to go on with his act. A militia officer like Cragg probably wouldn't know quite what to do about such a matter so it seemed right to go on playing a little stupid.

"Looks all right," he agreed dubiously. "What kin we do to help?"

CHAPTER 13:

Ober slid his identification back into its hiding place before he said slowly, "I don't reckon as how yo're much good fer me. I got to find Madison—and yo' don't know where he's at."

Kimbrell shrugged, guessing that he was still being tested. "Then traipse along with us fer a spell," he invited. "We'll be headed in the right direction. Sooner or later we'll git word about where's he's operatin' right now."

That seemed to satisfy the messenger—as Kimbrell had long since guessed him to be. "Mebbe I don't need to ride with yo'. I got two bits of information to pass on—and if'n it gets to Colonel Heffiner that's good enough. He'll let Madison know. But I also got a question to get answered. Mebbe you won't know the answer."

"Then mebbe you'd better handle yer own chores. I'm goin' to have me plenty troubles with these damned wagons we stole."

"Now wait a minute. You could save us all a lot of time—and I wouldn't be goin' back over these damned mountains in winter. Do yo' know how many men they've recruited up there in that place they call Mace's Hole?"

This time Kimbrell found it hard to keep his pose. He shook his head dubiously, using the gesture to steady himself. “Mebbe five hunnert. I ain’t been up thataway lately but that was the last I heard.”

“Hell! Yo’ folks was supposed to have a thousand! Heffiner claimed he could depend on that many.”

Kimbrell shrugged. “All I know is what I hear. Mebbe this Madison jigger got fooled. Things ain’t gone so well fer him, they tell me. A lot o’ loud talk and not much else. Our boys is the one’s what’s doin’ the job.”

“I’ll pass the word. Now here’s what yo’re to tell Heffiner—or Madison, if yo’ run across him. Get it straight now! Colonel Sibley’s fixin’ to take over from Baylor mighty soon now. He’ll have two thousand men all told. Give him six weeks to pound some discipline into his raw recruits and then he’ll make his move up the Rio Grande. He oughta be ready to take Fort Craig by mid-January but we’ll git another message through before that happens. The important part is that Heffiner’s crowd is to take this damned pass and hold it. Sibley don’t want nobody comin’ down outa Colorado Territory to mess up his plans. Yo’ got that?”

“Sure. That was the plan anyway, wasn’t it?”

“Right. But now you know about the time. The other message is about guns. Baylor got yore complaint about there not bein’ enough guns fer the recruits but he can’t do a damned thing about it. Even with what he got outa Fort Fillmore there ain't goin' to be enough for Sibley's men. He's got nothin' to send north even if there was a chance o' gettin' 'em through—but Sibley's got a suggestion. There's a lot o' extra muskets at Fort Garland. Sibley knows that from when he was still wearin' blue. Also there's some old carbines that was moved from old Fort Massachusetts. Somebody who knows the right people in this part of the country oughta be able to figure out some way to get a fake message to Fort Garland about sendin' them guns east. The Feds are movin' stuff all the time so it wouldn't stir up no suspicions if'n Fort Garland got orders like that."

Kimbrell grinned—but not for the reason that the other man thought. "Then our boys grab 'em along the trail? Right?"

"Right. A message from Fort Lyon would do the trick."

"Where the hell's Fort Lyon?"

Ober chuckled. "That's what the Feds is callin' Fort Wise. Seems like they didn't want it named for a Virginia governor so they named it after the Yank officer what got hisself killed at Wilson's Creek. Yo' know the place; the hell with what name it goes by."

They talked for another twenty minutes, Kimbrell getting nothing more in the way of useful information. Then he let the courier turn and ride back into the pass—much to the annoyance of Esteban and the men.

"Strategy," Kimbrell told them when it was safe to talk. "When he gets back to report they'll think their plans are working out. We'll try to make sure that we use the information for our own purposes. If we'd kept him as a prisoner they'd know what had happened and they'd find some other way to exchange messages. With winter getting close maybe they'll never find out."

A swirling snowstorm caught them that night and for the next three days the wagons remained in the Raton foothills. A long storm was not to be expected in November so prudence demanded that they wait it out rather than risk accidents on the slippery trails.

It turned out to be a dreary haul north to the Arkansas, bad weather making every day one of hard work and endless delays. Kimbrell began to worry about it. Business arrangements had to be completed with the post quartermaster, with William Bent, and with Indian Agent Boone. Then the empty wagons had to be moved back across the river to remain at Bent's stockade for the winter. There was no point in hauling them empty to Santa Fe so the only smart move was to leave them handy for any trade which might develop in the spring. Most of the men, led by Captain Vasquez, headed south when the wagons were stored, planning to use the long route and avoid the winter dangers of the pass. Kimbrell had to see to it that they were properly mounted and provisioned. That was a chore which Vasquez never seemed to understand.

It all took time. November was gone when Kimbrell with six wagons headed up the Arkansas. He had his regular four with him and Esteban had picked six men to remain as drivers. El Toro was to be cook for the party with the Ortiz boys as scouts. Pablo had arrived at Fort Lyon two days before departure time, reporting that his duties had been carried out.

Again bad weather plagued them but there was no real cause for alarm on that account. The same bad weather would also prevent much activity on the part of the enemy. The scheme could still work out neatly enough.

They slogged into Pueblo on the tenth of December, finding the town quiet. No one paid much attention to them and they halted without delay at O'Casey's cantina. While the barrels of Taos Lightning were being unloaded and paid for Esteban did a bit of visiting among the New Mexicans who drifted in to watch. He relayed his information promptly to Kimbrell. Zan Hicklin had been in town for a week, trying to buy supplies but without much success. There had been no sign of the supposed Confederates who had previously used the place as a part time hangout. Jonathan Ogden was very sick. There was a rumor that a fight had taken place in Raton Pass but no one seemed to know who had done the fighting.

"Hicklin still in town?" Kimbrell asked.

"Yes."

"Good. Maybe we've got a bite."

The wagons went on through to the Ogden place then, Kimbrell not feeling quite as cheerful as he had made himself sound. This next move was one he hated to make but he hadn't been able to figure out anything to take its place.

He sent three of the wagons directly into the corral, leaving the others outside for lack of space. Somewhat to his disappointment it was Mrs. Ogden who came out to meet him. They exchanged greeting and Kimbrell asked, "How is Mr. Ogden? I was told that he has been quite ill."

"Very ill," the lady agreed in a tight voice. He had already noted that her eyes looked tired even when she was giving him a smile of welcome. "I'm afraid the war news upsets him. Ball's Bluff and such things, you know."

He understood. At Fort Lyon they had been pretty disgusted at the Ball's Bluff fiasco. Men had died there along the Potomac for no good reason. Politicians with cheap commissions were blundering away both men and morale.

"You have supplies for us to handle?" she inquired, her tone changing as she switched subjects. Kimbrell guessed that part of the change was due to the fact that a bearded man in a long overcoat had just come into the corral. Zan Hicklin wasn't wasting any time.

"Mostly Taos flour and Mexican beans," he told her. "Just about right for local trade, I imagine." Then he added, mostly for Hicklin's ears, "We were plumb lucky to get the stuff through. Our boys had a brush with bandits comin' through the pass."

"So I have heard. Were you planning to leave the entire shipment in our hands?"

"Depends. A man has to make the best deal he can, you know."

The words were intended for Hicklin and they drew a quick response. A reedy sort of voice observed, "Sounds like a real rascal of a trader. That's what I like, a sharper what lets everybody know he's a sharper."

Kimbrell grinned as he turned to face the bearded rancher. He had known Hicklin a long time and knew his reputation as a smart rancher, a shrewd trader, the most incorrigible practical joker in the territory, and—as many claimed—the biggest liar. "So there's two of us," he agreed. "You aimin' to make me an offer?"

"Could be. Beans and flour, was it?"

"Right."

"I could use quite a bit of it. Got a lot o' hands to feed—or mebbe I shoulda said mouths."

He started to laugh at his own humor but

stopped abruptly as Kimbrell laughed, "Or maybe you shoulda said recruits. You're the Reb Quartermaster, I hear tell."

"That's a damned lie! I didn't—" He broke off again, bobbing his head apologetically in the direction of Mrs. Ogden. "Sorry, ma'am."

Kimbrell waved off the objection. "Have it your own way, Zan. I'm not particular about who buys the stuff or what his politics is. How much do you want and how much will you pay?"

This time it was Mrs. Ogden who began a protest but again Kimbrell interrupted. "I'm a tradin' man, ma'am. I make a profit when I can. The way this war's going I don't see that it means a thing to me except trouble. So I have to make up for losses where I can."

"You ain't been none too friendly to our boys," Hicklin complained.

"Was it your boys tried to rob me? I didn't ask questions about politics when gunmen tried to steal my stuff. So I don't ask questions when they try to buy it. That's fair all around, ain't it?"

Mrs. Ogden turned and left them at that point, her indignation clear. Kimbrell forced a grin and proceeded with the business of making a deal with Hicklin. It didn't take too long once the man understood that he could get what he wanted but only if he paid a premium price—and in hard money. They settled on a proposition which suited Kimbrell well enough. It gave him a nice profit—and would make him thoroughly hated by the Ogdens. Hicklin was to bring his own drivers and take over three of the wagons. Kimbrell even demanded and received a premium price on stock and wagons.

It took the better part of an hour to complete arrangements but in surprisingly quick time the three wagons were rolling west with their loads, Hicklin employees driving them. At that point Kimbrell left Esteban to work out the rest of the sale with the aloof Ogdens. He would retire to a nearby—and somewhat respectable—cantina with Hicklin to clear up details for further deals. It was Hicklin's proposal but Kimbrell had been ready to make it if the other man hadn't.

As he had foreseen, Hicklin tried to pump him as soon as they had downed a couple of drinks. He talked freely, knowing that everything he reported was already public. It was in the telling that he took care to strike a nice balance between anger at the way the war was interfering with business and ridicule at the way military affairs were going. Both sides were building up nuisance armies, he claimed. They weren't worth much at fighting each other. All they did was to turn out bandit gangs who could harass freighters. He poked fun at the pretenses of the Colorado troops and made grim jokes about the blunders of Federal commanders in the New Mexico forts. Then he turned on the Confederate heroes so bravely hiding out in the mountains.

By that time he was pretending to be slightly tipsy. "You got a stupid bunch, Zan," he confided to the rancher. "I know they're claimin' to be short o' guns but old Heffiner oughta know there's plenty o' guns at Fort Garland. Even the stupid Feds know that much. They're fixin' to move 'em before the winter's over. Need 'em back east, I reckon, or they think they do. Likely they'll just throw 'em away the first time the Rebs get 'em on the run."

He forced Hicklin to do a lot of questioning before he filled in the detailed facts. It wouldn't do to let the rancher feel that he was getting the story too easily. A man who prided himself on being shrewd had to feel that his own shrewdness was getting results. Finally, however, the whole story came out—in the form that Kimbrell wanted it. Hicklin now could hurry to Mace's Hole with the word that a Federal pack train would leave Fort Garland in January, moving during the winter because that was the time when less interference might be expected. The train would carry five or six hundred muskets and carbines now stored uselessly at the post. Kimbrell was not sure whether the guns would be taken to Denver or to Santa Fe. That part hadn't even been decided yet.

Hicklin left quickly after that and Kimbrell felt certain that the rancher was excited about what he thought he had learned. Now the important part was to keep anyone from doubting the yarn. If the Confederates believed the tale—and acted on it—their mystery regiment would be scattered around in the San Luis Valley watching for something that wasn't going to happen. They would have to watch the trails to Santa Fe and to Denver, in either case posting their men west of the Sangre de Cristos. They would be in no position to make any quick move toward Raton Pass or even to do any amount of raiding around Pueblo.

Kimbrell permitted himself a small glow of satisfaction. He believed that the scheme would work—but only if the enemy found no reason to become suspicious of him. Which meant that he still had a job to do. He had to continue playing the role of the cynical neutral, risking his secret with no one.

CHAPTER 14:

He found the three Ogdens together, evidently taking advantage of one of Jonathan's better days to get some book work done. The man looked ghastly but he was moving about. He was able to glare ominously at Kimbrell.

"Is it necessary for you to intrude here, sir?" he demanded abruptly. "We would prefer to deal with your agent."

Kimbrell didn't let his face betray any feeling. "You have no choice, sir," he said. "We have trade agreements and I am the trader."

"Trader or traitor," Ogden growled.

"Don't bandy words with him, Father," Alice warned. "We understand that he would deal with the devil if the price suited him. Let him have his say—so we can be done with the whole unpleasant mess."

Kimbrell had a feeling that she was more hurt than angry but he couldn't take much consolation in the feeling. "That's right," he agreed. "I'm not very popular here but there's business to be handled. Which of you is to play the martyr and get the job done?"

Ogden's reply was to stamp as vigorously as possible from the room. Most of the stamping came from his cane but the general idea was clear enough. He wasn't going to talk business with a traitor.

Alice hesitated only a moment and then she followed her father from the room.

Kimbrell grimaced as he found Mrs. Ogden's stare hard on him. "I kinda hoped it would be Miss Alice," he said quietly. "Maybe you'll understand when I tell you that none of this is what it seems to be. Better listen now so ease off with your mad while I talk fast. It's important."

He recalled that his first impression of the lady had been that she was pretty smart. Now he was glad to find her that way. She listened long enough to let him get a start and presently was nodding her belief and understanding. He explained that he had wanted to appear as a renegade in order for his story to be accepted by Hicklin. Nothing must interfere with that acceptance for at least a couple of months. By that time the rebels in the mountains should be dispersed in the San Luis Valley, unable to answer any call from an invasion army or to do any raiding east of the mountains.

"But you supplied them with food," Mrs. Ogden protested.

"Of course. Otherwise they might start raiding to get it. My whole aim is to keep them quiet and out of any trouble that may develop. Feeding them could be the best possible strategy." He went on to lay out the whole story for her, explaining even the Confederate invasion plan as he now understood it. "I found out about this because it was my job to find out," he told her finally. "I'm what enemy folks would likely call a spy—for Colonel St. Vrain and the New Mexico officials who had a hunch that military officers weren't being very alert. I guess you know what happens to spies who get caught. That's why I don't take many people into my confidence."

"I'm flattered," she said dryly. "Do you have any proof of this fantastic scheme you mention? What makes the Confederate leader think that he can undertake the conquest of Colorado?"

"Because he expects help from the men in the mountains." Again he filled in details. He had tried to avoid mentioning the bloody business in the Ratons, but there was no way to explain his own plans except to let her know why he was thinking as he was. So he told it all, concluding, "By this time Union headquarters in St. Louis should have the story. I'm hoping that they will have ordered the Denver regiment to take action right here where they are needed. My little scheme was intended to provide a delay until that can happen."

Her smile came pleasantly enough then. "You're quite a fellow, Sam Kimbrell," she said. "I'm glad you're on our side. I'll keep your secret."

"Thanks. You know what it means."

"I also remember that you would have preferred to trust Alice rather than her mother."

He knew that she was being good-natured about it so he simply grinned. "A man has to look ahead, you know. I got off to a mighty bad start with your daughter but maybe I can do better after a while."

She nodded, eyeing him with an interest which he hoped meant what it seemed to mean. "You didn't do so badly," she assured him. "I think I'm going to enjoy talking when the time comes."

A company of Colorado men arrived at Fort Lyon. They were well armed and provisioned but they were not in a class with the men McCall had commanded. They were undrilled, rebellious and generally resentful of their role as advance guard. Fortunately for Colonel McIntyre they were quickly followed by a scout company under Captain Hazard—and Hazard knew how to handle the collection of hard rock miners, gamblers, runaway apprentices and outlaws who made up the First Colorado.

Hazard also reported that Governor Gilpin had moved frantically after getting orders from St. Louis by telegraph. The main part of the regiment would be moving toward Raton Pass—by way of Pueblo. A small force would remain at Fort Lyon and another one would go to Fort Garland, thus satisfying General Canby's requests. There would even be a sweep of the Sangre de Cristos to get rid of the rebels supposed to be in hiding there.

"So they finally believe in my imaginary rebels?" Kimbrell asked quietly.

Hazard laughed. "Guess who convinced the Governor?"

"Not Lieutenant McCall?"

"Exactly. As soon as the word got around that you'd verified your guesses by intercepting that rebel courier Stan got real smart. He had already talked himself up as the great expert on the Arkansas Valley and the Sangre de Cristos. It didn't take much thinking on his part for him to add up what you tried to tell him and what now was official. Give him credit. Maybe they'd have believed your report about a Rebel regiment getting ready to join Sibley. Maybe they wouldn't. McCall's big mouth convinced everybody."

"And I suppose he's getting the job of going after the Mace's Hole boys?"

"Right. As *Captain* McCall."

Kimbrell shrugged. "Bigger idiots have drawn bigger jobs. Likely he'll do all right." He was thinking that now he could stop worrying about the Ogdens. Somehow there wasn't much consolation in the thought. By this time Mrs. Ogden must have told her husband and daughter the truth about Sam Kimbrell.

Hazard seemed to read his mind. "Don't start thinking about that Ogden girl, Kimbrell. I've got a chore for you. Maybe I'd better tell you that we know a little more about you than we did before. We had a message from Santa Fe. Old St. Vrain was mighty positive about you—and it looks like he was right—and so were you. Now we're depending on you. You've got to get the regiment through Raton Pass. We're to take and hold the south end until we find out what Danby is doing on the upper Rio Grande."

He moved out with his scouts a few hours ahead of Hazard's men, riding hard but with plenty of caution. There was always the chance that some part of the Mace's Hole regiment had already moved into the Ratons. An ambush of any kind had to be avoided.

Three days south of the Arkansas they knew that the Confederates had not made any move to take the pass. They met a federal courier who had come through with small difficulties. He reported that the pass had not suffered too much from the weather and that he had seen no sign of troops anywhere along the trail.

His official message was less optimistic. Sibley's column had made the difficult Jornada del Muerto march in efficient style, attacking Canby's outposts south of Fort Craig and then marching up the east bank of the Rio Grande to attack in strength at the Valverde crossing several miles north of the fort. There had been a desperate battle and the Union forces had withdrawn to the defenses of Fort Craig itself. Canby was shouting for help and the Confederates had a clear path to Albuquerque and Santa Fe.

"Sounds like we'll be going on to Fort Union," Hazard said grimly. "Can you take the whole regiment through the pass at this season, Kimbrell?"

"Not with any kind of baggage train."

"Mules?"

"Likely. Enough to carry hard rations and ammunition. We'd better get as many men into the pass as possible. They can clear away slides so that the main force won't be held up."

"Then let's get at it. When the old bible-thumper hears this latest tale he'll be drivin' everybody hard."

Kimbrell frowned. "Is Chivington in command now?"

"No. Colonel Slough holds the command but sometimes he must wonder. Chivington takes a lot into his own hands. But he gets things done, damn his guts!"

Kimbrell didn't reply. He had heard a lot about Lieutenant-Colonel John Chivington—and some of it he didn't like. The man had come to Colorado as Presiding Elder of the Methodist Church but earlier he had been mixed up with John Brown and Jim Lane in the Kansas fighting. He had joined the First Colorado as its chaplain but had pulled strings until he was its Lieutenant-Colonel.

"Don't worry about him," Hazard chuckled. "He can handle our hardrock bully-boys and make 'em like it. We need him." He laughed aloud as he added, "Sounds funny to have a parson bossing such a gang. Maybe you heard the tale about that soldier at Bull Run whose life was saved when a Reb slug hit the Bible he was carrying in his shirt pocket? Well, that ain't likely to happen with our crowd. It'd most likely be a deck of marked cards that would save any of our boys that way. But old Chiv can handle 'em."

A good half of the pass was cleared when the regiment was reported approaching. Hazard rode north to meet them, ready to argue against any attempt to enter the pass with wagons. Convincing Colonel Slough might turn out to be quite a task.

Kimbrell was awakened that night to discover that Hazard had returned with no less a personage than Chivington himself. The column had halted some miles short of the pass itself but Colonel Slough proposed to move in without delay. Chivington was to make the decision about the sort of baggage train which could be used.

The man was as big as his gaudy reputation. Even under the buffalo coat which swathed him it was obvious that he was immense. The dragoon boots which covered him to the thighs were just about the biggest boots Kimbrell had ever seen and the round face with its heavy mustache and fringe of whiskers were equally imposing. The man looked tough even with a ridiculous woolen scarf pinning down the sides of his gray felt hat.

"I suppose you're Sam Kimbrell," he announced loudly as he swung stiff-legged from his saddle. "Glad to meet a man with a grain of common sense. I've heard a lot about you. Now tell me about this pass." He made it sound pretty abrupt but he took pains to extend his hand as Kimbrell slid out of his blankets.

In the next twenty minutes Kimbrell developed considerable respect for Elder Chivington. The big man asked intelligent questions and insisted on getting answers which he understood. Through it all a sense of urgency was clear. Chivington recognized that an emergency existed and he proposed to do something about it.

Only when Kimbrell had a feeling that he had been pumped dry did the big man relax the pressure. Then, abruptly, a different kind of question came out.

"Do you know a man named Hicklin?"

Kimbrell grinned. It was easy to remember his last dealings with the rancher. "Quite well. Why?"

"Is he a Secessionist?"

"No doubt about it."

"Then why did you smile when I asked about him?"

"Maybe I'd better tell you the whole story. It's time somebody knew." He explained how he had used Hicklin in his attempt to immobilize the rebel recruits. To his surprise it was Chivington who laughed then.

"Now I don't feel quite so bad about Mr. Hicklin," the big man said. "He pulled a trick on us but I think we'll make him sweat for it." He went on to relate how Hicklin had appeared at a camp south of Pueblo, claiming that regimental foragers had stolen about a hundred head of his cattle. He had protested his loyalty to the Union, had accepted the usual warrants in payment for the beef, and had offered to guide the regiment through Raton Pass. That night Hicklin, the warrants and the cattle had all disappeared.

"Sounds like old Zan," Kimbrell commented. "I guess he didn't know that he no longer had recruits to feed in the mountains. They should be getting pretty well scattered by this time."

Chivington changed the subject quickly. "I'd better get back to the column. It's definite that we can't go through with wagons?"

"It is."

"You're the man who knows. I'll pass the word. Captain Hazard will continue to command the advance but he understands that you are to make the decisions. Satisfactory?"

"Quite."

"So keep us moving. It could be more important than we realize."

CHAPTER 15:

Kimbrell found plenty of reason to be glad that Hazard was with him as they probed through the snows of the pass. The Pikes-Peakers—as the men liked to name themselves—were as unruly a mob as the one Kearny had brought in the old war. They fought among themselves, malingered, stole rations and even mutinied. From his post at the head of the column Kimbrell saw little of the actual trouble but he heard almost daily of a company being herded along at gunpoint by guards who might become the mutineers on the morrow. He wondered how a regiment like this could fight a battle.

On one point he could feel some satisfaction. Dropping back along the line of march during an easy period he saw that the pack train was small and that it carried only bare necessities. Apparently Chivington had taken his advice.

For three full days they had to break trail where a thaw had turned snow into slush and then into ice. Hazard ordered a company of troops forward, having the men break trail in relays so as to keep the scouts from exhausting themselves with the chore. To Kimbrell's amazement the grumblers stopped grumbling. With a job to be done they simply buckled down and got at it. Kimbrell hoped that they would rise to occasion in the same fashion when fighting time came.

The climb to the summit proved to be the slowest and hardest part of the march. Then they began to find stretches of trail without any ice crust. A little later the temperature began to climb and the ice and snow became no problem at all. Men discarded their heavy coats for the first time.

At that point they were met by a courier, a teamster who had once worked for Kimbrell and who didn't mind pausing to gossip a little before riding on back to the commander. The message itself was brief and to the point. Colonel Paul wanted the First Colorado to make a forced march to Fort Union. The Confederates were already on their way to attack the fort, having taken Santa Fe.

"What do you think, Jake?" Kimbrell asked the messenger. "I can't believe Sibley has moved so fast. Is this just another worry message?"

The man grinned, showing toothless gums. "It ain't my job to coddle kernels, Sam. I git paid fer ridin' so I ride. But it ain't real likely that any kind o' army got from Fort Craig to Santa Fe so damned fast."

The next day another messenger arrived. Fort Union was receiving refugees and supply wagons evacuated from Santa Fe. There were now details of the Union blunder down the river, but the picture remained much as it had been told earlier. Canby had let Sibley get around him. Now it remained to be seen whether the Union commander would make some attempt to hit the enemy rear. Sibley was actually in a trap if Canby would make it one.

For Kimbrell the disturbing part about the new message was that it mentioned a company of the First Colorado as having escorted refugees and wagons out of Santa Fe. Obviously McCall's company had not remained long in the San Luis Valley but had moved south to Santa Fe in time to become part of a retreat from that city. Kimbrell didn't like what it implied.

Two hours later he got his first look at Colonel Slough. The commanding officer apparently had decided that he would not depend so completely on Chivington so he rode forward himself, accompanied by a couple of staff officers who looked as rough as their men. Captain Hazard attempted something by way of introduction but Slough waved it aside. "I know this is Kimbrell. He's the man who knows this miserable country. Kimbrell, can we get to Fort Union before the enemy does?" He wasn't as loud as Chivington but he was more abrupt.

"I can only guess, sir. I think we've got plenty of time."

"I don't want guesses, damn it!" This time he let his voice take on extra volume.

Kimbrell knew how much strain the man had

been under so he didn't let himself get annoyed. "Call it calculation then. I figure on road conditions, distance, the condition of Sibley's men and animals after that long march up from El Paso. We'll make it in plenty of time."

"Good. Now tell me how many men it will take to defend Fort Union."

"Fort Union can't be defended. It's not a fort in the first place, only a guard barracks along the Santa Fe Trail. They added a star fort last summer when they realized that the main part of the post could be hammered to bits by a couple of guns placed on some commanding bluffs. It's no help. The new fortifications are a mile away from supplies and water. The place couldn't be defended against a good strong Indian attack!"

"Then it's a hopeless matter?"

"Not at all, sir. The place to defend Fort Union is along the trail from Santa Fe. An enemy column might be stopped there, perhaps even in a smart ambush."

"Can we get that far?"

"I think so. I've got a strong hunch that we've been hearing a lot of scare talk but no real estimate of the situation. We'll make it."

"I hope you're right. It's up to you. Make the best pace possible."

"We'll do that, sir. And I'd like to ask a question. Were any of your men left at Pueblo to defend against raiders there?"

"No. We brought every available man."

He swung away without giving Kimbrell a chance to say anything more. Actually, there was nothing to say—nor was there anything to be done. The big danger was in front. Unless every effort was made to halt Sibley's victorious troops it wouldn't make any difference what the Mace's Hole rebels did around Pueblo.

The southern slopes proved easier and the advance set a hard pace, holding up only when more mutinies in the column delayed the march. Kimbrell began to feel the lack of sleep. He was driving hard for long hours but at night exhaustion still wouldn't let him get his mind away from his worries. Every hour was taking him farther away from his real concerns and he had the fear that this whole expedition might prove to be another fiasco. It didn't seem possible that this wrangling mob could hold together long enough to face an enemy. Even if they managed it he didn't see how they could be changed from a mob into a regiment in time to do a decent job. It seemed like a waste of time and effort to get them through to New Mexico.

Then another messenger brought evil tidings. Colonel Paul had decided that Fort Union could not be defended. He planned to evacuate the post, burning all supplies which his troops could not carry away. His regulars, a company of cavalry and three of infantry, would march south in an effort to join General Canby who was supposed to be following Sibley north. The six companies of New Mexico Volunteers would be sent home.

Slough appeared once more at the head of the column. "How far to Fort Union, Mr. Kimbrell?" he demanded without preliminary.

"Sixty, seventy miles."

"I'm ordering a forced march. We can't afford to let that idiot destroy supplies. We're already on short rations."

Kimbrell still did not believe that Sibley's force could be within striking distance of Fort Union but that was not the big problem now. "Set it up for your men to follow," he told Slough briefly. "We'll set a good pace."

"I've already issued orders. Cooked or hard rations only. The best mounted men take the lead, others to remain behind with the mules and the remount detachment. Stragglers will be dropping out, I suppose, but they can catch up later. I want some part of this regiment in Fort Union just as soon as you can get them there!"

The pace had scarcely been speeded when the lowering clouds brought a driving mixture of sleet and rain. Men who owned ponchos put them on, the others simply turning up the collars of their buffalo coats to get as much protection as possible. The temperature plummeted and the rain turned into a driving snow. By nightfall they were riding through a howling blizzard but they kept right on riding. Men dropped out but others moved up to take their places. Nobody seemed to be doing much prodding. For once the Colorado men didn't need any.

Darkness brought a fresh problem. In this comparatively open country many side trails broke away from the main trace, inviting a mistake that might cost hours. Kimbrell and Esteban stayed with the lead riders at all times, trying to avoid that kind of error. Mostly they rode in silence, Kimbrell with his nagging worries about what might be happening back on the Arkansas, Esteban respecting the silence because he understood its meaning.

Mostly the men were walking now, saving their horses and at the same time keeping warm. By midnight Hazard commanded only thirty men, less than half of them from his own company. Kimbrell had eight of his scouts.

Fortunately the snow never became heavy. It swirled across the trail, blinding men whose eyes were already inflamed from loss of sleep but it did not block the trail.

Kimbrell passed the final six hours of darkness in a half-dream. Sometimes he thought he had actually slept. When the first streak of a gray dawn brought an end to the snow he was almost afraid that he had gone to sleep and taken a wrong turn. No landmark seemed familiar. Only after he had talked briefly with Esteban could he believe his eyes. The advance had covered better than forty miles in that grueling battle against the storm. The whole thing seemed more unbelievable when he topped a rise and got a look at the column of men behind him. The regiment was coming. As far as he could see riders were in an unbroken line. The First Colorado was showing its mettle now that the chips were down.

More hours passed. More miles fell behind. Esteban dropped out of line to talk with a Mexican farmer who came out of his adobe to stare. He reported back that the man had heard of no trouble at the fort. No militia had been seen. Obviously Colonel Paul hadn't yet started abandoning the post.

The weather turned fine as the morning wore on but now the sun was as hard on the eyes as the snow had been. Kimbrell stopped figuring on the passage of time. All that mattered was to keep moving. The men behind him were doing it; he had to set them a good example.

Suddenly—and it came as a surprise even though he had been watching his landmarks—he realized that he was staring at the sprawling structures which made up Fort Union. The place looked almost peaceful. Maybe that was why it didn't seem quite real to him.

Disbelief grew as he saw that the garrison was being mustered for a formal reception, lines of blue-clad men forming along the edges of the parade ground with other men in partial uniforms lined up behind them. For a post supposed to be in a critical condition this one was getting mighty fancy.

Some of the reason behind it became apparent as he pulled aside to let Colonel Slough and his staff lead the march into the post. Colonel Paul was putting on a show because he had become host to Governor Connelly after that official fled from Santa Fe. Connelly and Paul made welcoming speeches—while the half dead Colorado troopers slid from their horses and went to sleep on the ground. For men who had endured the hardships of that brutal march out of the Ratons this was sheer nonsense. Kimbrell didn't wait to see where the anger would erupt first; he simply headed for the nearest building which looked like a stable, motioning for his scouts to follow. All he wanted was a pile of hay where he could get some sleep.

When he awoke again it was daylight and he thought that he had slept through part of the afternoon. Then he realized that he was not sleepy any longer so he decided that he must have slept through the night and into the following morning.

He didn't try to sit up until he had gotten a few thoughts together. His first movement drew a chuckle from a bundle of something near him. Other bundles were all around and he knew that New Mexicans and Coloradans alike had followed him to the stable. It was Esteban's rather precise English which caught his ear now. "There is no hurry, amigo. Nothing happens."

"How long was I asleep? It's tomorrow, I suppose?"

Esteban chuckled again. "It is tomorrow, yes. All of us sleep like dead men except the commanders, I understand. Captain Hazard tells me that they do not rest because they fight among themselves."

"Where's Hazard? Where's McCall? What's the news on Sibley's army?"

Esteban had no answer for him on any of those points. The squatty man had been awake twice since arriving at the post but had been able to learn nothing that seemed to be important. All he knew was that the Colorado men had been most of the night in straggling in, the rear guard with the pack mules and the spent animals not arriving until after dawn. Meanwhile the first arrivals had stirred up plenty of trouble. They had resented being kept in ranks for welcoming speeches and they threatened mutiny when rations were delayed. More than anything else they resented having made a forced march for no good reason. Fort Union and everyone in it was their enemy. One gang broke into a sutler's store and cleaned it out. Since a lot of the loot consisted of wine and whiskey the next moves became pretty violent. Drunken brawls spread through the post and spilled over into the off-post hangout which housed some of Santa Fe's gaudiest females. By midnight the stockade was full of drunken prisoners, most of them bruised and bleeding. Then the Provost stopped making arrests and let them raise their particular brand of hell as they saw fit. Fort Union couldn't handle them. Colonel Paul had already stated that he would have preferred Sibley's Texans to arrive at the post first.

Captain Hazard came into the stable while Esteban was making his whispered report. Most of the other men in the place were still sleeping but a few had roused themselves to listen. They seemed pretty sober and Kimbrell guessed that these were refugees from the rioting which must have taken up the whole night.

"No better at headquarters," Hazard told them as he caught the final statements from Esteban. "Slough has called Paul a fool and a coward. Paul wants our men out of the post—before they wreck it. Which they're likely to do, I'm afraid. They're still looting unchecked although our officers are trying to get them under control. That's not why I came over here, however. I thought you'd want to know that our good General Canby—who hasn't stirred out of his fort to chase Sibley—is issuing orders again. Colonel Paul is ordered to defend Fort Union and to give up any plans for evacuation or the destruction of supplies. Now

Paul and Slough can wrangle about how the job can be done."

"Which I suppose they'll do. Seems like most officers can't get around to fighting the enemy because they're so damned busy fighting each other. Where's McCall?"

"Out on patrol. I gather that he has been up to his usual mouthy tricks. Colonel Paul thinks he's a boy wonder so he's using McCall's company as pickets on the Santa Fe trail."

"What happened in the San Luis Valley?"

"Nobody seems to know. McCall is claiming credit for having dispersed a whole regiment of Confederate militia up that way. That's part of the reason Paul thinks so highly of him, I reckon."

It was a full week before Kimbrell could learn anything definite. Meanwhile he had to wait and worry. There was no possibility of starting a march northward, either alone or with any of his men. Their horses and mules were exhausted and he could not make any deal for fresh animals. There was nothing to do but to wait while officers wrangled, men rioted and messengers continued to come in with conflicting reports.

Finally Kimbrell got a summons from Chivington. The big man looked worried and angry after the days of bad feeling at headquarters but he controlled himself well as he motioned Kimbrell to a chair.

"I want you to do another job for us, Mr.

Kimbrell," he said almost formally. "I suppose you know what our situation is here?"

"I've heard the usual rumors. No sign of Sibley yet. The war is being fought in the family."

Chivington grimaced. "We're about done with that, I'm glad to say. Colonel Slough has just realized that he out-ranks Colonel Paul. From now on he is assuming the command of all forces available here."

"Fine. Now nobody needs me. I've got government contracts and a lot of wagons waiting for me at Fort Lyon."

"And a personal interest at Pueblo, I understand." The big man's smile became just a little too benevolent as he added, "You also have an interest and a duty here. It was your warning that let us prepare for this emergency. You have played a major role in following up that warning. I think you ought to see it through. There will be little delay from now on."

Kimbrell shook his head. "I'm not looking for credit. It's your war now. I just want to get my men back to their wagons."

"Now that is a big part of the problem, my friend. Your men happen to be enlisted personnel of the Third New Mexico Scouts. At the moment most of them are on duty with Captain Vasquez under the general command of Colonel Chavez. They are keeping a close eye on Sibley's movements. I can't let you take them."

"Then I'll go alone."

"To drive wagons? Come now, Kimbrell!" He was really doing the preacher-politician act now. "Stop worrying about Pueblo. I happen to know that the rebel force—which you had so much trouble getting anybody to believe in—has been disbanded. The men have decided that this war is not for them. They'll be back on their farms by this time."

"You are sure of that?"

"It's official. Now let me get on with my proposition. We need you here, not only because you have shown us that your advice is good but also because you get along well with Mexicans. Most of our officers don't. Help us through the next couple of weeks—until we defeat Sibley—and I promise that you can start north at once—with your full company."

"You think two weeks will do it?"

"Perhaps less. Our plans are made. We will march out within twenty-four hours. Colonel Slough is adopting your proposal to meet the enemy along the trail. I think you'd better go along with your own plan."

"Two weeks," Kimbrell agreed. He didn't like to think what might happen along the Arkansas in two weeks but he didn't have much choice.

CHAPTER 16:

Kimbrell saw only the beginning of the preparations. He went ahead with Captain Hazard who took temporary command of a mixed detachment of scouts. Hazard's orders were to join up with both McCall and Vasquez, then to place the combined force under the command of Colonel Chavez—if Chavez could be located. One way or another the detachment was to locate Sibley's column definitely.

Finding McCall proved easy. The big redhead had set up a camp at the western fringe of a grubby little collection of sheep pens and mud huts known as Las Vegas. A tent beside a crumbling adobe appeared to be his headquarters, uniformed men on duty as sentries and an orderly.

"*General* McCall, apparently," Hazard muttered as they approached and saw the big man standing in the open fly of the tent. "Maybe Colonel Slough is going to have another fight to see who's boss around here."

"Funny thing," Kimbrell told him. "It was McCall who said something about how a man thinks he's a soldier if you give him a gun. Some men think they're officers if you give 'em a shoulder strap."

"And knock out their brains!" Hazard growled.

"It's gettin' so I kinda hate to admit bein' an officer."

Kimbrell laughed. "Cheer up. Officers in New Mexico don't shape up any worse than any other kinds. They've just been getting more chance to be stupid."

McCall broke up the exchange, hailing sharply as they came within earshot. "Ain't yo' got yo'self in kinda bad comp'ny, Cap'n? Yo' seem to be ridin' with the same Kimbrell what sells grub to the enemy—and sends 'em off to steal guns outa Fo't Gahland." It was obvious that he felt the accusation should stir up a lot of excitement.

Instead Hazard simply grinned at Kimbrell. "Shall we tell the sonofabitch, Sam? Or do we let him be the loudmouth four-flusher for a bit longer?"

It was fun to see the big fellow sputter and then do his usual job of finding a new line of attack. That was one thing about McCall. He was smart enough to know when he was barking up the wrong tree and not too proud to do some crawling in finding another tree. Today, however, Kimbrell didn't feel like watching an exhibition of the sort. "We'd better get down to the facts," he said shortly. "There's a war to be fought."

He had slid from the saddle as he spoke. Now he sketched in his whole story, beginning with his commission to find out the truth about Colorado. He could see that McCall was having trouble swallowing some of it but Hazard's occasional nod carried him through those sections. Finally it was Hazard who summed it up, "He was right about the Rebels. He called the turn on this invasion. He brought our boys through the pass in time. Chivington thinks he's a mighty big man. You'd better keep that in mind unless you want to come to blows with Chiv."

It took a while for McCall's story to come out, even with Hazard prodding him every time he tried to defend himself for some action which didn't really need defending. McCall's men had seen evidence of Rebel activities as soon as they began to work across toward the San Luis Valley but they had not run across any large groups until they were almost at Fort Garland. Then they had struck a camp which evidently had been set up for the detachment which was watching for the expected movement of guns. There had been a brief fight and the Rebels had been sent flying. McCall's men had captured three prisoners, all of them young fellows who had gotten pretty disgusted with their adventure as Rebel recruits. They admitted that they had tried to desert but didn't dare after they were sent out on the patrol job. They were always too short on rations to risk starting on a ride of any length.

The prisoners had been taken to Fort Garland, arriving there at about the same time that Canby's request for help came in. The fort's commander was in a quandary. He didn't have men enough to defend the post from any sort of real attack but he was being asked for troops to be used in New Mexico—and he had an organized enemy in his own back yard.

The Fort Garland officers had not understood the entire situation, not even guessing that a ruse had been employed to keep the enemy recruits out of action, but they had hit on a ruse of their own to dispose of what appeared to be a threat to the fort. They had told the prisoners that Sibley had been badly defeated on the Rio Grande. Then they had released the men, giving them a friendly tip to get themselves and their friends out of the war before they found themselves in real trouble.

"Ah laid it on mighty thick," McCall reported, some of the boastful tone coming back. "Yo' know how Ah feel about it so Ah give 'em mah best Mississippi talk about lettin' rich bastahds fight theah own wah. Ah don't figgah as how that Reb outfit is goin' to be no trouble to nobody from now on."

"I hope you're right," Kimbrell said grimly. "If you just busted 'em up and left gangs of guerillas loose to plunder the country—" He didn't need to finish. The others knew what he meant.

"Nothing more to be done about it now," Hazard cut in. "McCall, I'm in command of scouts until we find Colonel Chavez. You'd better fill me in with what you know so far."

The redhead nodded. If he resented losing his temporary authority he didn't show it. Producing a rough map he ran a big finger along the curved line of the trail. "Santa Fe is oveh theah. Road cuts south in a big loop to stay cleah o' the mountains. It don't quite miss 'em all. Right heah, mebbe fohty miles west of us, theh's a pass. Glorieta Pass, they call it. Trail goes through Apache Canyon. That's the place we oughta take."

"It's a lot closer to Santa Fe than it is to us," Kimbrell commented. "I'd think Sibley would have it by this time."

According to McCall's best information there were no Confederate troops in the pass. Sibley and about half of his army were still in Santa Fe, trying to recruit local militia, gathering supplies—or perhaps merely delaying because Colonel Sibley had old friends there. A strong detachment under a Colonel Scurry had started toward Apache Canyon with some field guns escorted by cavalry but all reports indicated that only an advance guard had reached the western approaches to the pass. There was still time.

Hazard issued his orders promptly. Word went back to Chivington who was commanding the advance units. McCall's fine headquarters was abandoned and all scouts were ordered to converge on the eastern mouth of the canyon. Perhaps the combined scout companies could hold the pass until Chivington and his cavalry could arrive.

They found Vasquez and the main part of the Third New Mexico Scouts at a ranch near the eastern mouth of Apache Canyon. The rancher—known to most people only as Pigeon—because of his vaunted skill in doing the Pigeon Wing at frontier dances—agreed with Vasquez that only a small force of Confederates were at the opposite end of the canyon. Chavez and his men had been using the canyon for handling reports until two days earlier. Now the only messengers who came through were being forced to use a trail across the mountains that was known only to a few of the local people. Still the facts seemed clear. The Confederate advance had halted at the far end of the pass. There was still an opportunity to take the strategic summit.

They moved out at dawn of the day following receipt of the orders, knowing that the job needed to be done without delay. Chivington and his advance units were reported to be only a few miles away. They should arrive at Pigeon's ranch long before the scouts could return.

Vasquez led the way along a sort of goat trail until they reached the point where he had earlier turned back. There the faint trace almost disappeared and they had to search carefully to find passages across ledges and through clumps of jackpine. A stretch of relatively open country where boulders and juniper were the only obstacles let them pick up speed a little, but then they had to go back to the dreary business of clawing a precarious way through broken rocks and along ledges where every step threatened disaster. The only consolation was to feel that there was little likelihood that an enemy force would ever make use of this trail.

Finally they knew that they were on a downgrade. Kimbrell's sense of direction told him that care was doubly important now. They must be moving down toward Johnson's place, the ranch which had been located near the western opening of the canyon—much as Pigeon's ranch was at the eastern end—and which was where the Confederate advance was supposed to be in camp. Probably Confederate scouts would be out. Certainly there would be sentries posted somewhere above the canyon.

Kimbrell conferred with Vasquez and called a halt. Then he went forward with only two of the men, moving with the greatest of caution. No alarm must be given. If the Confederates hadn't learned of this path there was no point in calling it to their attention.

Suddenly the canyon was in front of them. They were looking straight down on Johnson's ranch—and the Confederate camp. Few men appeared in view but the rest of the picture was interesting enough. Wagons were everywhere.

Three field guns with their caissons were parked near huge stacks of supplies. Sibley hadn't been wasting his time, no matter how the reports made it sound. He was getting ready for a big push.

The part which bothered Kimbrell most was the lack of men. Only a few sentries lounged beside the supply area. Obviously the troops who had been reported waiting here had moved into the canyon. Those sentries would not be so careless unless they knew that they had somebody between themselves and the enemy.

Kimbrell moved twice to make sure that he had seen all there was to see, then he motioned to his men and started back. There were possibilities in the situation. Chivington ought to know about it.

The afternoon was well spent when he joined Vasquez once more. A return to Pigeon's ranch in the darkness seemed to be out of the question so they made camp in a stand of jackpine and talked it over.

At dawn they moved out, following the plan they had come up with before taking to their blankets. Men were left in pairs at strategic spots along the trail, particularly where time had been lost in finding a passage. In the event that any attack were to be made across this mountain track it would be important to avoid loss of time. Guides would be mighty useful. And they could also serve as outposts in case the enemy attempted a flanking operation of the same kind. The latter possibility now seemed remote but it had to be kept in mind.

The return was almost as slow as the original march had been but Kimbrell didn't mind too much. His men were now placed so that they could lead other men across without delay. He and Vasquez were alone when they began the descent of the goat trail which led to Pigeon's ranch. That was when they heard the distant rumble of cannon. The fight for Apache Canyon had started!

At the ranch they found everything surprisingly quiet. The only troops in sight were guards who had been left with supplies and extra stock. Their commander reported that Chivington had marched his whole command into the canyon at daybreak and the only report which had come out was that he had the enemy on the run.

This cheerful note altered abruptly as fleeing men began to appear. Their stories were hopelessly in conflict but when whole companies began to appear, still in formation but definitely retreating, it became clear that something had gone wrong. A few prisoners and some wounded only added to the contradictions. Chivington's appearance brought some show of order but a new element of confusion was added when two companies of Colorado cavalry arrived with Colonel Slough leading them.

The first angry words between the two officers told Kimbrell that this was no time for him to be making any direct reports about the mountain path and what lay at its other end. Anyway, Captain Hazard had ordered the reconnaissance so the report should go to him. He found Hazard without delay, swapping the report for an account of what had happened in the canyon.

Boiled down to essentials, the story was one of wasted opportunity. Chivington had marched his column to the summit of Glorieta Pass and had met the enemy's advance there. At first his strategy had been excellent and the Confederates had fled, leaving many casualties behind them. Instead of pressing a pursuit Chivington had seemed to lose his head, paying more attention to prisoners and his own casualties than to the task at hand. He had let the attack come to a halt and the enemy had used the time to bring up a couple of field guns. The guns had done no damage, being badly aimed, but then opening fire had sent the infantry into full retreat.

Chivington had rallied the Colorado troops but had failed to press the fight, even though his scouts on the canyon walls told him that one good charge would disperse the small enemy force around the guns. At that point the Confederate commander had sent a white flag forward, asking for a truce to pick up casualties. It was a bald effort to gain time but Chivington had agreed.

Then he had abandoned the entire field to the enemy.

"The old buzzard got carried away by your talk of how this would be the fight that could save the West," Hazard told Kimbrell. "He thought he saw his chance to be a national hero. So he pushed ahead without waiting for the rest of the command—and now he's in trouble. Slough will make him sweat for his blundering!"

He nodded toward the ranch house where the two officers had gone to finish their argument. "Might as well get over there and tell them about the mountain trail. Maybe it'll take their minds off of what they're calling each other."

He was gone for nearly two hours. In the interval more troops came in from the east and Kimbrell realized that most of Slough's column had been pushing hard to reach the scene of trouble. Maybe something could still be salvaged out of the opening disaster. It would have to be done quickly, he was certain. Sullen talk was sweeping the camp as the men who had been in the canyon tried to hide their own failures under complaints about bad leadership. They were angry enough to fight well if someone would only give the right orders promptly.

Such orders came with surprising promptness. Slough was to make a new attack in the pass a little after dawn but Chivington was going to start well before that time and try to get in position to hit the enemy's rear. Sibley's advance was to be wiped out between the two Union forces. This was the big opportunity to smash the ambitious Confederate schemes.

Kimbrell liked the sound of it but he also liked a report which Hazard passed on to him. Scouts from Fort Lyon had reported that a strange column was moving out of the Sangre de Cristos across toward Raton Pass. All indications were that the Rebel recruit regiment was still intact, apparently still intending to give Sibley some assistance. Colonel Paul had sent men from Fort Union to hold Raton Pass against them.

"Seems like Ah didn't fool 'em much," McCall observed, coming up in time to hear the substance of the account. "Mebbe Ah'm glad. Ah keep thinkin' about what Kimbrell said about guerillas and Ah didn't like what Ah was thinkin'. Mebbe yo' gents don't know it but some day Ah'm plannin' to git me back to Pueblo. That gal at the tradin' post was mighty purty."

Hazard laughed suddenly, shooting a quick glance at Kimbrell. McCall misunderstood the reason for the laugh. "It ain't funny," he declared angrily. "Yo' and Kimbrell didn't pay her much mind, Ah know, but there's some as don't think about business all the time. Ah wouldn't want to think about her gittin' mixed up with no guerillas."

"Not even with militiamen," Kimbrell said, his face expressionless.

CHAPTER 17:

Chivington's force moved out two hours before dawn four hundred strong. Each man had strict orders to keep in touch with the man directly in front of him and to keep moving. There was no other way to get so large a column through such rough country. Kimbrell led the way, accompanied by Colonel Chavez who had brought part of his scout detachment in during the night. For the first time since joining the Colorado regiment Kimbrell felt a sense of excited anticipation. This could be the big strike of the campaign.

The march went well, the relays of guides leading the column swiftly through areas which had taken a lot of slow searching on the previous trip. At dawn they were close to the summit and by mid-morning men were listening for the sounds of firing which would mean that Slough's column had gone into action. Once Kimbrell thought that he had heard the muffled roar of cannon but he could not be certain. At noon they reached the spot where he had halted his men on the previous day. Chivington promptly began to deploy his men for the attack while Chavez and two scouts went forward to reconnoiter. For once there was no lost motion. Everyone seemed to know what had to be done.

The assault force was in position when Chavez returned with the word that the enemy evidently had been reinforced during the night. At least two hundred men were at the supply camp so it seemed certain that additional forces would now have come face to face with Slough's advance.

Chivington didn't hesitate. He signaled the advance, each company having been assigned to an approach route which would keep them under cover as long as possible. The idea was good but McCall fouled it up when he tried to move his company with drill commands. A sentry gave the alarm and Chivington roared the command for a general assault.

Riflemen from one of the New Mexican companies promptly opened a wild but evidently disconcerting fire on the wagon camp and the Confederates fled. A few of them tried to take cover among the wagons but mostly they ran for horses and got away, some into the canyon but the majority headed toward Santa Fe. The fight was over before the Colorado troops could get to close quarters, three defenders dead and two captured. There were no casualties among the attacking force.

Chivington wasted no time in bewailing the lost opportunity to bag prisoners. He simply set his company commanders to the task of destroying everything in sight, giving McCall's company the ugly task of killing the horses and mules. The order served as a reprimand. "See if you can do the job by squads and platoons!" he snapped.

Hurried questioning of the prisoners disclosed the fact that Colonel Scurry had arrived during the night and was now facing Colonel Slough with about seven hundred additional troops. Sibley was supposed to be on the way out from Santa Fe to press the fight.

Fresh orders were issued promptly. "Kimbrell, start your men back across the trail right away. I want them to move fast. Set up the same kind of guide relays. We'll need them after dark. Captain Hazard, move the men out as fast as they've done their jobs. We've done all we can do here; there's no point in being caught between two forces which both outnumber us. We'll fight a rear guard action, if necessary, but nothing more."

Kimbrell relayed the orders to his men and led the way up the mountain again. The rank odor of burning bacon filled the canyon and some of the ammunition wagons were beginning to explode. He saw that the Confederate cannon were being spiked and their wheels knocked off. McCall's men were shooting animals or cutting their throats. Huge flames marked the spot where some sixty loaded wagons were going up in flames. Maybe Sibley's army had not been much damaged but his prospects of continuing a campaign had been dealt a hard blow. What had happened to Slough's men in the canyon was something the raiders could worry about while they struggled through the rocks on the return trip.

The scouts made good time, setting up their relays only when they reached the part of the trail which the returning troops would cover after dark. The rest of the trail was pretty well marked with recent usage. Kimbrell knew that the first companies were not far behind when he began the descent to Pigeon's ranch. Chivington had passed the word forward that they were to form at the top of the goat path, letting Kimbrell scout the ranch. In case things had gone badly for Slough there might be a chance of retrieving some of the loss by a night attack. The men were weary but they would recognize the need for such an effort.

The desperation attack wasn't necessary. Kimbrell heard enough to know that Pigeon's ranch was still Union headquarters so he sent the word back and moved on down to be challenged by a Colorado sentry. There were wounded men getting attention near the fires but the camp didn't seem to be under any great strain. Apparently Slough hadn't been hit too hard by the combined Confederate forces.

It didn't take long to find out what had happened. Slough's men had marched toward Glorieta Pass with the full expectation of smashing a Confederate force that had already been badly hurt by Chivington. Instead they had met Scurry's advance and had been forced to retreat under heavy fire, both sides suffering many casualties. In the midst of retreat Slough had tried the same trick which the enemy had used on the previous day. He had asked for a truce.

To his amazement the request had been accepted—and then the Confederates had made a quick retreat. No one had been able to guess at why the victorious enemy had decided to withdraw but now it seemed clear that Scurry had received word of the attack on his supply base. The fleeing men who had brought the information most likely had exaggerated the strength of the raiders and Scurry had swung to fight his way out of what had seemed like a trap.

Men continued to come down out of the mountains as the night wore along, Chavez and his scouts appearing just before McCall's blood-smeared company arrived. They agreed that the Confederate retreat toward Santa Fe had become almost a panic. The destruction at Johnson's Ranch had done something to the morale of the invaders. Sibley was now in a lot of trouble. His troops were short of ammunition and supplies—and he had a Union army under General Canby blocking his normal supply line. The threat to Fort Union seemed to be definitely ended.

Kimbrell had anticipated just such a report. Throughout the night he had fought off his own fatigue to make arrangements for heading north, even getting an order from Chivington that would permit his men to get fresh horses at Fort Union. Vasquez would return to Santa Fe as soon as the town was clear but the other twenty members of the crew ready for travel would head for the Arkansas. Whether they would go directly to Bent's Fort and the wagons was something that would have to be decided later.

For the first few days Kimbrell forced himself to restrain his impatience. His own fatigue reminded him that he was asking a lot of men who had done so much hard riding. Too much haste now might mean big trouble later. He used the remount stop at Fort Union to give the crew some extra sleep, the formalities of military requisition making the delay a necessity. Another lengthy halt came when they reached the northern end of Raton Pass. Colonel Paul's men still held an outpost there but their patrols could find no trace of any force moving against them. Kimbrell talked to every man who had done patrol duty but none of them had seen any sign of the Mace's Hole regiment.

On the following morning they met a patrol which had spent some time scouring the country northwest of the pass and this time they got some answers. The patrol had seen plenty of sign and they had talked to a Mexican trapper who had a shack in the foothills. The trapper declared that several hundred men had camped in thick timber not far from his shack but had suddenly left, only a day before the patrol appeared. Most of the men had ridden north but perhaps fifty of them had moved straight back into the mountains as though they planned on going to Taos by way of remote mountain trails.

Kimbrell's eyes went wide as he listened. He was still staring into the distance when he asked, "What do you make of it, Esteban? Am I thinking straight?"

The New Mexican displayed the broken teeth in his usual grin. "Am I to know what you think, amigo?"

"You always do."

Esteban seemed to be reciting a lesson. "These men learn that their army has been defeated. They have no reason to stay. Many would have gone home months ago except that their leaders persuaded them of duty. Now they have no duty so they go. A few decide to remain with Heffiner and Madison as the leaders ride to join Sibley on his retreat. That is what you think?"

Kimbrell chuckled dryly. "You say it better than I think it. Anything else?"

"Perhaps we should ride to Pueblo instead of to Bent's Fort. There are some of these men who do not go home or to their mines."

"Our business is at Bent's Fort."

"But we go first to Pueblo. No?"

"We go first to Pueblo. Yes. Business can wait."

Less than a day out of the Ratons they verified most of their guesses. A rancher whose son had elected to ride with Heffiner had sent word home by one of the men who had seen all he wanted of the war. Since the rancher had been opposed to secession in the first place he wasn't slow to condemn the men who had tried to bring war to the territories. He was disgusted at his son's choice but otherwise he welcomed the news he had received. There would be no more fighting in Colorado, he predicted.

Kimbrell wasn't as optimistic. As his party moved north they found the tracks of many small groups, apparently recruits heading for their homes, but then they ran across the trail of a larger party. Eighteen horses. Esteban claimed that they all carried riders. Generally Esteban was right. It was what Kimbrell had been fearing. So many men riding together suggested trouble.

Again the guess was soon confirmed. Just before sunset they talked to a New Mexican sheepherder whose hut had been visited by the eighteen. They had remained all night at his place, keeping him under guard while they killed his chickens and forced his wife to cook for them. Then they had taken all of his food supplies and his only two horses. They had been gone since early morning.

Esteban questioned the man at some length but

could learn little more. The herder spoke only Spanish and the bandits had conversed in English. He had heard no names and knew nothing of their plans. He did recall that the leader was a younger man with a prominent chin.

"Old lantern-jaw!" Kimbrell exclaimed. "Cragg's sidekick. Pretty much the same gang that tried to grab our wagons. I think we'd better push on tonight. I'd like to catch up with them before they reach Pueblo."

They knew that they were gaining when they picked up the trail next morning but they were still a half day short of the Arkansas when they saw that their quarry had split up. Three men had continued on toward Pueblo but the other fifteen had swung to the west.

"I can't figure what it means," Kimbrell growled. "Unless they're headed for Zan Hicklin's place—and I don't think he's backing any bandit gang." He didn't care very much. The best part of it was that only three men were riding toward Pueblo.

He led his men across the Arkansas just before dark, alert against the possibility of ambush. The town seemed silent, no one appearing on any of the streets near the river. Kimbrell issued his orders quickly. They would move in with flanking parties out, ready for attack. It seemed a bit melodramatic but it made good sense.

Nothing happened until Kimbrell and six men

were directly in front of the Ogden place. Then the front door opened just enough to permit a rifle muzzle to appear. Alice Ogden's voice came in a strained but determined tone. "Stay away from here! I'll shoot the first man who tries to dismount!"

Kimbrell didn't move a muscle although there was still light enough for him to see that the rifle was not pointed at him. "Take it easy, Miss Ogden," he called out. "We're not as bad as we look. I'm Sam Kimbrell."

He could hear the little gasp of surprise. Then the gun disappeared and the girl stepped into the doorway. "Will you come in, please?" she asked, her voice shaking a little as though the relief from strain had been too much for her.

"Of course." He was sliding from the saddle as he replied. "Is there trouble in town that my friends ought to know about before we make any moves? Things seem mighty quiet."

"People are afraid. They're staying indoors."

A yelp of joy from a nearby alley told him that someone else had recognized the newcomers. Now he didn't need to press his questions on Alice. Esteban would soon have all of the answers.

"It's Father," the girl told him in a whisper as she led the way into the trading post. "I'm afraid he is dying."

A lamp burned in a wall bracket near the corner

table and in its yellow gleam he could see the blanketed form of Jonathan Ogden on the floor. A bandage covered the man's head and came down across one side of his face. Mrs. Ogden knelt on the floor by her husband's head, applying some sort of antiseptic to the uncovered scratches on his face.

Kimbrell nodded briefly and hunkered down to feel for a pulse. It was weak and irregular, like the injured man's breathing. Ogden was alive but little more than that. "What happened?" he asked in a whisper.

Mrs. Ogden motioned toward the other side of the big room. "Alice can tell you—over there. If he can hear, he'll only get excited." Then her husky whisper became a stronger tone as she said, "I was praying that you would come, Sam Kimbrell."

He nodded again and rose to follow Alice to a far corner. "Your mother explained about me?" he asked.

"Months ago. And we heard about you from one of the Colorado officers when they came through here. All of us misjudged you—but we understand now. What is the news from the south?"

"Seems like the Colorado troops did the trick. But more about that later. What happened here?"

She told it in some detail although he had a feeling that she was skipping over parts which were distasteful to her personally. A huge hulk of a man had come to the post a little after noon and had stalked around as though taking an inventory, refusing to pay any attention to the Ogdens when they tried to find out what he wanted. He had been a little drunk but he had been more smug—as though he was greatly pleased with what he had in mind. Finally he had stopped directly in front of Alice, swaying a little as he stared at her. He had said something about her being his particular cut of the loot. That was when Jonathan Ogden had ordered him out of the place. The fellow had promptly knocked Ogden into the corner of a counter, breaking his jaw with the blow and causing him to suffer a serious head wound from the fall.

She told it steadily, only breaking a little when she described the attack on her father. Kimbrell patted her shoulder awkwardly, wanting to do more but knowing that he had to keep his wits about him. A vicious pattern was beginning to come clear. Perhaps time was already running out.

"Had you ever seen this man before?" he asked.

"I'm not sure. He seemed to be familiar with the store."

He told her hastily of what had happened south of the Ratons and how the Confederate regiment had disbanded. "I think this gang is planning a campaign of terror. I also have a hunch it's made up of men who used to hang around here last fall. Might you have seen him at that time?"

"I believe I did! I think he was in here with Mr. Hicklin once."

He turned toward the door. "Do what you can to help with your father. I won't be far away." Then he was hurrying out into the gloom of the early evening.

CHAPTER 18:

He was just in time to find Esteban and Mike O'Casey dismounting in front of the trading post. Esteban blurted out a report in such haste that Kimbrell understood the urgency of it right from the start. Just before noon three riders had come into town from the south. They spent almost an hour in a careful search of the streets and alleys but then they had proceeded to rob three of the cantinas, killing one owner who protested. Then they had separated, ignoring the few frightened people who remained in sight. One had gone to Ogden's while another had gone to O'Casey's. The third had made a survey of warehouses and storage sheds.

"Scouting," Kimbrell muttered. "That's the way I had it figured. They sent three men in to see whether any troops might have been left here by the Colorado regiment. Now the rest of the crowd can come back and plunder the places their scouts tell them are worth hitting." He was thinking about what the big outlaw had said to Alice Ogden but still he kept his voice down. It wasn't too easy.

"That ain't near half of it!" O'Casey exclaimed. "The bastard what busted in on me got drunk enough to spill the whole damned yarn. They ain't plannin' to plunder this town; they're plannin' to wipe it out!"

Kimbrell stared in the darkness and O'Casey seemed to read the doubts in the silence. "Lemme tell ye about it," he hurried on. "Them three bastards was part o' Ed Craggs crowd when he was helpin' recruit that Rebel outfit in Mace's Hole—which I didn't know about at the time. Ed useta claim that fittin' up militia outfits wasn't no way to fight a war out in this country. When he got drunk enough he'd lay out real neat about how the job could git done."

"Now these men plan to do what Cragg proposed a year ago," Esteban broke in excitedly. "I have talked to many people who now come out of their houses and wish to run away. They agree. Pueblo is to be destroyed."

"That's the way of it," O'Casey agreed. "I got my warnin' to git out. This fella Clint what was at my place got a real loose tongue when he'd put down three or four good wallops. This gang thinks Cragg had the right idea—only he made the mistake o' tryin' for a Kimbrell wagon outfit instead of a helpless settlement. Now they're gonna work things out the right way—while there ain't no troops around."

He went on to fill in details as he had learned them. The lantern-jawed man, known to O'Casey as Arkie, was now the nominal leader of the band but there was a hint that Gooley—or some such name—might try to take over the command. Gooley was the burly man who had gone to the Ogden place. One way or another, the plan was to make Pueblo an example of terror. They would wipe out the town in such a manner that everybody within hundreds of miles would fear their operations. Then they would strike again, probably at Bent's Fort because it would give them extra reputation to destroy a well-known place that was just across the river from Fort Lyon. People would forget that neither spot was defensible. All that would be remembered was that Colorado guerrillas had done the job. After that recruits would flock to join the band. Towns would pay tribute to avoid being hit. Colorado would be a cinch. They wouldn't even get into trouble if troops were sent against them. There were plenty of places to hide until it would be time for another strike. A whole regiment had gone undetected for months; a band of guerillas would have no trouble.

O'Casey had more of it but for Kimbrell that was quite enough. Time was running out. The three outlaw scouts had seen how helpless the town was. There were few able-bodied men in town and only three of them owned weapons. The raiders would believe that no resistance could be made.

"What have you done so far?" Kimbrell asked.

Esteban had been taking action. The Ortiz

boys and another freighter had gone out to act as sentries. They had orders that one was to come in with word of the enemy's approach. They must take steps to make sure that they were not seen. Two would stay away from town, ready to pick off any fleeing survivors of the attack party.

"You're reading my mind again," Kimbrell said grimly. "We'll get them all if we can." He assigned men quickly, covering warehouses which might attract looters and the saloons which certainly would be prime targets of the gang. Then he placed his few remaining men around the Ogden place. In all cases the men were warned to remain under cover no matter how the fight went. There would be no way of telling friend from foe in the uncertain light. By having all defenders holding to fixed positions it would be safe to assume that anyone who moved was an enemy. He didn't need to tell any of the men that this was to be a fight of extermination. They had heard enough to know that they were about to meet a gang of mad-dog killers.

Careful preparations took most of the time which Esteban calculated was available. Moonrise would see the attack party on the move, he felt sure. Kimbrell made one final arrangement before he turned the outside pattern over to Esteban. The password "Glorieta" was to be used in case anyone had to make an emergency move. There was no time for more planning. He had to get back to his preparations for defending the Ogden store. Two men went with him. No more were available with the other positions properly manned.

He knew when he reentered the place that Ogden had died during his absence. The lamp had been moved to a different bracket but there was still light enough for him to see that the blanket now covered the bandaged head. Alice and her mother stood near a window, evidently trying to recover some part of their composure.

"Sorry," Kimbrell said shortly. "It's a bad time to force more trouble on you but you'd better hear what I've got to say. There's not much time."

"No need to coddle us," Mrs. Ogden told him, her voice almost steady. "We have a pretty good idea of what you are going to say. The gang is coming back."

"That's it." He made it as brief as possible, still explaining how the various reports had brought the threat of danger into focus. "We think they will attack as soon as there is moonlight. Less than an hour. I'm afraid we won't have time to do anything about . . . Mr. Ogden . . . until later." He was motioning the two New Mexicans to their posts as he spoke.

"What can we do to help?" Alice asked. "There must be something. We have two revolvers."

"With ammunition?"

"Of course."

"Then you can reload. One of you work with me and the other with Francisco there at the front window. I'll take the door. Bring the guns and we'll make sure that you know how to do the job. You'll load all six cylinders, of course. At a time like this we won't bother with an empty."

It pleased him that Alice came to take her place with him while her mother joined the New Mexican. He had to spend a little extra time with her because the two guns were of different makes and calibers. "Keep the cartridges in separate piles," he warned. "You'll have to work in the dark so be sure you know which kind go with each gun."

"All of the percussion caps are alike?" she asked.

He grinned faintly. "I guess you know what you're doing. Just keep as cool as possible—and don't get into the line of fire."

"I think you have more confidence in me than I once had in you. Father and I were quite ashamed when we learned the truth about you."

"It was my fault. I thought I had to play it that way. When did your mother tell you?"

"In January. Then we had a letter from Governor Gilpin. It was a confidential account of how you had alerted the authorities to something they didn't even suspect. He asked that we be ready to help, if we could, but not to talk about it. I felt very superior when that asinine Captain

McCall stopped here and was doing his bragging about how he had been responsible for all of the things we knew you had done."

Kimbrell had to grin at the memory of McCall's avowed interest in Alice Ogden. "McCall's a good man when he keeps his mouth shut," he said shortly. "Which he almost never does."

Hoofbeats in the distance brought the whispered conversation to a halt and Kimbrell stepped out into the beams of a rising moon just in time to hear Esteban's hoarse warning to the other men. "Nobody fires! That's our man coming in." Evidently the squatty man wasn't taking any chances on any of his troops being too literal with that order to shoot anything that moved.

The rider was Pablo Ortiz and his message was exactly what they expected it to be. Kimbrell saw to it that Pablo's horse was hurried into the stable while Esteban assigned the youth a post and repeated the orders to him. Kimbrell issued a final warning to the men within earshot. "Don't fire until you're sure. We think it's the enemy coming in but we don't want to make any mistakes." Then he hurried back to the doorway where he could hear Alice relaying the word as to what was happening outside.

"Time to get rid of that light," he told Mrs. Ogden as he went in. "Take your posts and get ready. Remember to stay down and out of the line of fire."

She made a brave attempt at a smile. "See that you do the same, Sam Kimbrell. We're depending on you for so much."

They had scarcely gotten ready when they could hear riders coming. Hoofbeats and a babel of loud voices hinted that the raiders scorned any attempt at caution. This was to be a massacre of helpless victims and none of the attackers cared whether the victims were warned or not. Kimbrell didn't need any reminder. He still remembered what had happened to the cantina owner, to Ogden—and the sheepherder's wife. The herder had not spelled it out but every man in the party knew the truth.

The voices came closer and presently a few words rang out above the general din. Kimbrell knew that he was listening to the lantern-jawed man, the one O'Casey had called Arkie. "What the hell!" the man bellowed. "I told you the gal was your'n, Gooley, but I didn't say you could keep her! The rest of us ain't made a' wood, you know."

"Don't try to welch on me, damn you!" a heavier tone retorted. "Or mebbe you'll wish you *was* made o' wood—so you wouldn't bleed!"

"We'll talk about it later," Arkie said hastily. "Tonight's all your'n. Let's git on with what we got to do."

Kimbrell could feel the girl's shiver as she pressed against him. "Makes me wonder," he whispered in her ear. "Now I don't know which one I want to shoot first."

"You can shoot more than once," she told him, her voice grim even in a whisper.

"Thanks for reminding me. Now get back away from this door."

He could see them by that time. The whole gang had come to the Ogden place. Now he had to face odds. He hoped that the opening guns would even things up a bit.

The lead riders halted in front of the door and he took dead aim at the one he thought was Arkie. It was a hard choice, feeling as he did, but somehow it seemed to be the thing to do. Then he squeezed off his shot, ducking almost to the floor in order to get under the smoke cloud before he fired his second slug at the broader target which he guessed was Gooley.

He believed that he had scored hits with each shot but there was no time to keep score. Firing had broken out from the rear as soon as his first shot opened the fight but the nearer outlaws didn't seem to realize that the shooting behind them was enemy fire. They slid from their horses and tried to rush the door of the trading post. Kimbrell emptied his gun, knowing that Alice was counting aloud while he fired. With the sixth shot she had the other gun almost in his hand.

He took it and pushed her back to safety. Slugs were crashing into the woodwork around him but he held his position and kept driving slugs of his own into every shadow that moved. Suddenly none of them were moving.

Somewhere at the corral excited Spanish yells sounded and somebody shouted, “Glorieta, they escape! Two of them!”

Riderless horses plunged in all directions but no human figure moved within Kimbrell’s range of vision. He stepped out through the doorway and a gun blasted at him from ground level. He felt the slug pull at the side of his shirt but he fired once at the flash before jumping to one side. Then he hammered away at the sprawled shadows in the street, firing grimly, methodically, trying to make sure that there would be no more desperation shots from dying thugs.

Other gunfire from the corral gate told him that his men were taking his example and were making certain that there would be no wounded prisoners. It made him a little sick to think about it but he issued no order to change matters. This was the way it had to be.

The racket stopped in time for him to hear Esteban’s questions. The squatty man was checking casualties among his men. There were none. The attackers had been wiped out without the defense getting a scratch. Kimbrell let his fingers probe at the hole in his shirt and found no blood. They had been mighty lucky.

Three distant shots sounded then. Esteban

yelled in triumph. "The business is ended! Pedro and Guttierez have finished them. They would not miss."

"Not quite ended," Kimbrell told him as he walked gingerly between sprawling objects to where Esteban had appeared. "We must remove all traces of what happened here tonight. By tomorrow these dead men must have disappeared. Then we will have quiet funerals for Mr. Ogden and the cantina owner."

"It is important to do it that way?"

Kimbrell smiled faintly in the darkness. "For once you do not read my mind, amigo. I think we should do exactly the opposite of what these bandits planned. They wanted to destroy a town so as to let everyone fear more violence and murder. They planned to use the story as a means of scaring other people into doing what they wanted. It is the kind of thing I've been trying to block ever since the war started. I think maybe we keep any talk from getting a start. Perhaps that will avoid future violence and fear. Let the people of Pueblo know that this is to be their secret. By keeping the secret perhaps they keep the peace—and the town becomes a sign of peace instead of a sign of dread. No one will then try to avenge any of these men because no one will know what happened to them."

He knew that Alice had come up behind him in time to hear his words. Now the girl moved closer to put a hand on his arm. "I am ready to agree with Mother," she murmured. "Mother thinks that you are a very smart man."

Kimbrell stared down at the dark shapes in the moonlit street. Then he thought about that other form on the floor of the trading post. There was still some pretty grim business to be handled. "I'm smart enough to know that this is no time for me to say the things you make me want to say."

She let her fingers close briefly on his arm. "There will be other times," she said softly. "Better time, I'm sure."

Center Point Large Print
600 Brooks Road / PO Box 1
Thorndike, ME 04986-0001 USA

(207) 568-3717

US & Canada:
1 800 929-9108
www.centerpointlargeprint.com